SO-AAL-417

## A Note from Stephanie about
## Playing It Cool

I know you shouldn't brag, but I really wanted to impress Michael, the cool new boy in school. He just moved here from Los Angeles and he knows tons of famous people. So naturally, I told him I know famous people too—like a rock group that would write a special song for our school video project. The only trouble is, I don't know any famous rock groups! And there isn't any special song. Soon Michael—and everyone in school—will think I'm the most un-cool kid around. How will I ever get out of this mess?

But enough about my problems. Let me tell you about something that *isn't* a problem, like my family. My very big family.

Right now there are nine people and a dog living in our house—and for all I know, someone new could move in at any time. There's me, my big sister, D.J., my little sister, Michelle, and my dad, Danny. But that's just the beginning.

Uncle Jesse came first. My dad asked him to come live with us when my mom died, to help take care of me and my sisters.

Back then, Uncle Jesse didn't know much about taking care of three little girls. He was more into rock 'n' roll. So Dad asked his old college buddy,

Joey Gladstone, to help out. Joey didn't know anything about kids, either—but it sure was funny watching him learn!

Having Uncle Jesse and Joey around was like having three dads instead of one! But then something even better happened—Uncle Jesse fell in love. He married Becky Donaldson, Dad's cohost on his TV show, *Wake Up San Francisco*. Aunt Becky's so nice—she's more like a big sister than an aunt.

Next Uncle Jesse and Aunt Becky had twin baby boys. Their names are Nicky and Alex, and they are adorable!

I love being part of a big family. Still, things can get pretty crazy when you live in such a full house!

**FULL HOUSE™: Stephanie novels**

Phone Call from a Flamingo
The Boy-Oh-Boy Next Door
Twin Troubles
Hip Hop Till You Drop
Here Comes the Brand-New Me
The Secret's Out
Daddy's Not-So-Little Girl
P.S. Friends Forever
Getting Even with the Flamingoes
The Dude of My Dreams
Back-to-School Cool

Available from MINSTREL Books

For orders other than by individual consumers, Minstrel Books grants a discount on the purchase of **10 or more** copies of single titles for special markets or premium use. For further details, please write to the Vice-President of Special Markets, Pocket Books, 1230 Avenue of the Americas, New York, NY 10020.

For information on how individual consumers can place orders, please write to Mail Order Department, Paramount Publishing, 200 Old Tappan Road, Old Tappan, NJ 07675.

# FULL HOUSE™
## Stephanie

## Back-to-School Cool

### Devra Newberger Speregen

A Parachute Press Book

A MINSTREL® BOOK

PUBLISHED BY POCKET BOOKS

New York   London   Toronto   Sydney   Tokyo   Singapore

The sale of this book without its cover is unauthorized. If you purchased this book without a cover, you should be aware that it was reported to the publisher as "unsold and destroyed." Neither the author nor the publisher has received payment for the sale of this "stripped book."

This book is a work of fiction. Names, characters, places, and incidents are products of the author's imagination or are used fictitiously. Any resemblance to actual events or locales or persons, living or dead, is entirely coincidental.

A MINSTREL PAPERBACK *Original*

 A Minstrel Book published by
POCKET BOOKS, a division of Simon & Schuster Inc.
1230 Avenue of the Americas, New York, NY 10020

A Parachute Press Book
Copyright © 1995 by Warner Bros. Television

FULL HOUSE, characters, names and all related indicia are trademarks of Warner Bros. Television © 1995.

All rights reserved, including the right to reproduce this book or portions thereof in any form whatsoever. For information address Pocket Books, 1230 Avenue of the Americas, New York, NY 10020

ISBN: 0-671-52275-2

First Minstrel Books printing August 1995

10  9  8  7  6  5  4  3  2

A MINSTREL BOOK and colophon are registered trademarks of Simon & Schuster Inc.

Cover photo by Schultz Photography

Printed in the U.S.A.

# Back-to-School Cool

# Chapter

# 1

◆ ◀ ◾ ◆

Brrrinnnnggg!

Stephanie Tanner groaned when she heard the bell. She looked at her best friends, Darcy Powell and Allie Taylor, and said, "Well, that's it, guys. Summer is officially over. Eighth grade has just begun."

Stephanie opened her locker and checked her reflection in the tiny mirror inside the door. She flicked her blond bangs until they fell just right, then slammed the locker shut and turned back to her friends. "Allie, Darcy, tell me again where the summer went," she said.

Allie slumped against the row of lockers. "I don't know," she sighed. "But it seems like only yesterday we were swimming in Darcy's pool, talking about guys and eating pizza."

1

Stephanie punched her friend playfully on the arm and said, "Reality check, Allie. That *was* yesterday!" Allie and Darcy were the best friends Stephanie had ever had—Allie since kindergarten and Darcy since the sixth grade, when her family had moved to San Francisco from Chicago. The girls had spent most of the summer together—swimming, going to the mall and the beach—it had been a total blast.

Allie chuckled and twisted a long lock of her wavy brown hair. "Still, summer vacation flew by."

"I know what you mean," Darcy agreed. "Now here we are, back in these dark, dingy hallways, dressed in school clothes, carrying brand-new notebooks and pencils, and facing a whole year of studying!"

"Well, I guess there's one good thing about going back to school," Stephanie said. "You get to go shopping for new clothes. I love that skirt, Darcy."

"Oh, thanks," Darcy said. She was wearing a short red-and-black pleated skirt and a red sweater, which complemented her dark skin and bright eyes. "My dad asked me if I quit school and joined the army when he saw these new boots," she added with a laugh.

"Doesn't sound like a bad idea," Stephanie said. "At least you don't get homework in the army."

"And the food's probably better than the cafeteria stuff they feed us too," Allie added.

"Don't remind me," Stephanie said, slinging her brand-new backpack over her shoulder. Her dad always bought her a brand-new backpack each September. This one had lots of pockets in it for little things like pencils and gum.

"So who do you guys have for history?" she asked.

Darcy pulled her class schedule out of her notebook and checked. "Ms. Shapot," she replied. "Third period."

"I have Shapot second period," Allie told them.

Stephanie groaned. "And I have her fifth. It figures, the three of us don't have one single class together!"

"Well, we both have media skills first period," Allie offered. "Darcy, maybe you can switch in."

Darcy shrugged and glanced at her watch. "Maybe. But right now I'd better get to homeroom. The second bell's going to ring any minute."

"I can't believe it," Stephanie moaned. "Summer's really over!"

Allie covered her ears with her hands. "Stop! You're totally depressing me!"

Darcy's eyes suddenly lit up and she smiled an

enormous smile. "Hey, I know something that will cheer you up!" she said.

"What's that?" Stephanie asked.

Darcy tossed her black curls as she leaned closer to her friends. "There's a new kid in school!" she whispered.

Stephanie made a face. "So?"

"So, it's a new *guy!*" Darcy replied. "And he's really cute!"

Allie smiled. "Now, that's interesting! Tell us more."

Stephanie laughed. "Spill your guts!" she ordered Darcy.

Darcy clutched her books to her chest. "Okay, here's the scoop. He was on my bus this morning. His name is Michael Allen. He just moved here from L.A. He's in eighth grade, and he has first period media and fifth period math."

Stephanie's eyes narrowed. "How do you know all this about him already?"

"I peeked at his schedule on the bus," Darcy said with a sly smile.

Stephanie laughed. "Is there anything you *don't* know about him?" she asked.

"Yeah, like what's his favorite food?" Allie joked.

"Peanut butter and jelly," Darcy replied. "Anything else you'd like to know?"

Stephanie and Allie stared at her in disbelief.

Darcy shrugged. "He was eating a sandwich on the bus," she explained.

Stephanie cracked up. "Boy, Darcy, did you ever think of becoming a detective?"

"Ha-ha. Anyway, he's a total babe!" Darcy said.

Stephanie and Allie exchanged excited glances.

"Excellent!" Stephanie said.

Bbbrrrinnnggg!

Darcy pouted. "That's the second bell. Gotta go. See you guys at lunch."

Allie frowned. "I guess we should go too," she said to Stephanie.

"Yeah, let's hurry!" Stephanie replied. She had a huge grin on her face.

"Hey, wait a minute. Why are you in such a rush?" Allie demanded. "It's the first day of school. Summer's over!"

"But media class will soon be starting," Stephanie called over her shoulder as she ran down the hall. "And then I can see this new boy for myself!"

After homeroom Stephanie rushed to her first class and took a seat in the front row. She was actually pretty excited about taking media skills. It

5

was the most popular course in school and only eighth-graders could take it. Stephanie remembered how her older sister, D.J., had talked about it all the time when she was in junior high. Back then Stephanie thought she'd never be an eighth-grader, but now, here she was, one of the "upperclassmen" of her school.

Mr. Merin, the media teacher, stood up and welcomed the eighth-graders to his class. He was one of the coolest teachers in school, Stephanie thought. He told a lot of funny jokes, and he always wore jeans to class on Friday.

He went on to describe some of the projects they'd be working on that semester. The class would be broken down into groups, and each group would do something different, like put together a magazine, make a video, or even create an entire advertising campaign.

Stephanie flashed a smile at Allie, who sat on her left. "This class sounds awesome!" she whispered.

Allie nodded eagerly.

Stephanie glanced around the classroom. Everybody was paying attention. They all seemed pretty psyched about the projects too. But Stephanie didn't see the new guy that Darcy had told them about anywhere.

Stephanie was about to whisper to Allie again,

when the classroom door opened. Immediately, all heads turned toward the door.

"Oh, yes, come in, Michael," Mr. Merin said with a smile. "Class, this is Michael Allen. A new student. He's just moved here from Los Angeles."

Stephanie's jaw nearly hit the floor. All she could do was stare at Michael. He was taller than most eighth-grade boys and had long light brown hair that fell to his shoulders. He wore faded jeans that were ripped perfectly in both knees, and a black leather jacket. Darcy had said he was cute, but "cute" hadn't even begun to describe him. Michael Allen from Los Angeles was the most gorgeous guy Stephanie had ever seen in her life!

Mr. Merin pointed to the empty chair on Stephanie's right. "Michael, why don't you take that seat next to Stephanie Tanner. I was just telling the class about their first project."

Stephanie couldn't believe her luck! Her mouth was still hanging open as Michael fell into the chair beside her, and she couldn't take her eyes off him. All she could do was stare at his adorable dimples and perfect profile.

Michael let his backpack slide down his arm and fall to the floor. Then he pushed his hair off his face and smiled at Stephanie.

"Hi," he said with a lopsided grin.

Stephanie's heart melted. She felt her face turn red and was sure she would die of embarrassment—right there in the front row of media skills. But somehow she managed to get hold of herself and return his greeting.

"Hey," she mumbled.

Mr. Merin walked over to his desk and shuffled a batch of papers from side to side. "Talk quietly among yourselves for a moment," he instructed the class. "I have to complete Michael's paperwork, then I'll get back to assigning the projects."

Immediately everyone began talking, laughing, and whispering. Stephanie wanted to talk to Allie, but she couldn't take her eyes off Michael. To her surprise, Michael began to talk to her.

"This class looks cool," he said to her. "Mr. Merin seems really nice."

Stephanie nodded. "It is," she replied. "He is." *Get a grip, Tanner,* she said to herself. *You can come up with something longer than a two-word sentence.*

Michael gazed around the room, then back to Stephanie. "So you're Stephanie Tanner," he said.

Stephanie's eyes widened. *Wow! He knows my name!* she thought with delight. "How did you know that?" she asked.

Michael pointed to Mr. Merin. "He just said—"

8

Stephanie chuckled nervously. "Oh, right. I forgot."

There was a moment of awkward silence, then Michael leaned in very close to Stephanie, so close that she saw he had the most beautiful hazel eyes she'd ever seen. Hazel with tiny flecks of gold in them. So close, that she could reach out and touch him. So close that she could even imagine . . .

"Do you have an extra pen?" he asked.

Stephanie blinked twice and jumped a little in her seat. "A pen?" she repeated. "Oh . . . sure, a pen."

Her heart pounding, Stephanie turned around and pulled her backpack off her chair. When she did, she noticed that every girl in the class was staring at her and Michael. Happily, she dug a pen out from her bag.

"Here, Michael," she said extra loud so they'd all be sure to hear. "So when did you move to San Francisco?"

"Two weeks ago," Michael replied. "I'm going back to L.A. this weekend for my uncle's wedding. He's a big movie director, you know."

"Really?" Stephanie asked. "In Los Angeles?"

Michael nodded. "Uh-huh. He knows Arnold Schwarzenegger and Steven Spielberg."

"Wow!" Stephanie said, impressed.

"I want to become a director too," Michael went

on. "My parents bought me this really awesome video camera for my birthday last month."

"Oh, yeah, I have one of those," Stephanie said, hoping to impress him. Actually, the camera was her uncle Jesse's and she'd never even used it. Jesse didn't want anyone going near it. He'd explained that it was "sophisticated equipment and not a toy," but most of the time he used it to film his five-year-old twins doing something like having a tea party with the dog.

"Is it eight millimeter or VHS?" Michael asked.

Stephanie swallowed nervously. She'd never even heard those terms before! "It's, uh, eight millimeter," she replied uneasily.

Michael's eyes widened. "Awesome," he said with a grin. "My uncle has an eight millimeter too. My camera is VHS."

Stephanie smiled and nodded. She was trying frantically to think of something intelligent to say when, thankfully, Mr. Merin stood and cleared his throat.

"Okay, kids. Listen up. I'm going to divide you into small groups and assign each group a media project. Now, I realize having a project assigned to you on your first day back may come as a shock to you," Mr. Merin went on, "but I like to jump right into things. Of course, I'll be working closely with each group to answer your questions and show you how to use your media tools correctly."

Stephanie hoped she and Allie were in the same group. Then they'd have a great excuse for doing their homework together. Stephanie's father always insisted she do her homework by herself, but if she and Allie were assigned to work together, her dad couldn't argue. She held her breath as Mr. Merin called out names.

"And the last group," Mr. Merin announced, "will be the video group. Now, don't get all crazy on me here. I promise that everybody will get a chance to use the video equipment. Each month we'll switch project groups so you'll all get a chance to do everything. The following students will make a video documentary as their first class project. Tanner, Taylor, Volpe, and Washington."

Stephanie smiled at Allie. Whenever anything was done alphabetically, she and Allie got to be together. In fact, that was how they met in the first place. Back in kindergarten they were seated right next to each other—Tanner and Taylor.

"Excuse me, Mr. Merin," Michael said, raising his hand. "What about me?"

Mr. Merin gazed down at his notes. "Oh, sorry about that, Michael. Why don't you join the video group?"

Michael smiled at Stephanie. "Great," he said.

Stephanie returned the smile, then leaned back in her chair as Mr. Merin talked more about the class projects. *Oh, yeah,* she thought to herself. *This is going to be one awesome semester!*

When the bell rang to end class, Michael followed Stephanie and Allie out to the hall. "Maybe I could come over after school and see that camera of yours," he said to Stephanie.

Stephanie shuffled on her feet nervously. Jesse was awfully protective of his camera. But what could she do? The cutest guy in school—no, make that the cutest guy in the whole world—had just invited himself to her house! "Yeah, great. No problem," she said.

"Tomorrow afternoon?" Michael asked. "Then we can talk about the project too."

Stephanie hesitated. Then she noticed four girls from media class were huddled across the hall, listening to every word. She had to admit, all the attention felt pretty great. "Tomorrow would be perfect, Michael!" she quickly said.

"Well, I should go," Michael said. "I don't know my way around the building yet and I have to find the science lab."

"Two lefts and a right," Stephanie said with a smile.

Michael flashed his perfectly white teeth. "Cool, thanks!"

Stephanie and Allie watched as he made his way down the hall. But before he turned the corner, Michael spun around and called back to Stephanie.

"Don't forget about our date tomorrow, Stephanie!"

Stephanie heard the girls across the hall gasp. She smiled and waved back to Michael.

"I won't!" she called out. Then, still waving, she whispered to Allie, "Catch me, Al! I think I'm going to pass out!"

# Chapter
## 2

◆ ◂ ◾ ◆

"A date?" Darcy asked. "A real date?"

"No, no, not a date," Stephanie said. "Michael just asked me if he could come over tomorrow to check out my camera—I mean, Jesse's camera."

"You should have seen your face when he asked you!" Allie said with a laugh. She took two oatmeal-raisin cookies from the box, then passed them to Darcy. The three girls had all headed over to Stephanie's house right after school to compare notes on the first day back.

"From what Allie says, you were redder than a stoplight!" Darcy added.

"Okay! Okay! Are you guys going to tease me all afternoon?" Stephanie got up from the kitchen table and swung open the refrigerator door. She took out a bottle of apple juice and poured three glasses.

"I know I was blushing," she said. "But he's just so incredibly cute! Every time he asked me something, I felt my face turn red. He probably thinks I'm a real dweeb."

"No," Darcy assured her. "Not a dweeb. A geek maybe, but definitely not a dweeb!"

Allie laughed. "If he thinks that, then why'd he make a date with you?"

"That's what I'm trying to tell you!" Stephanie protested. She passed a glass each to Allie and Darcy, then joined them at the table. "It's not a date! He just wants to come over to see my video camera."

Darcy took a sip of juice, then put down her glass. "What video camera?" she asked.

Stephanie groaned and put her head in her hands. "The one I told him I had. The one that I really don't have, so maybe he shouldn't come over tomorrow after all."

"I'm very confused," Darcy said. "Do you have a date with Michael, or don't you?"

"Okay," Stephanie said patiently. "For the hundredth time, here's what happened. Michael was saying he wanted to become a movie director and that his parents bought him a video camera. Then I said I had one, one with eight millimeters—"

"With eight what?" Allie interrupted.

Stephanie gazed at her friend. "You mean you don't know either?"

Allie just shook her head and shrugged.

"So he said he wanted to come over and see it, and I said sure," Stephanie finished. "That's it. The big date. End of story."

"So what are you going to do when he asks to see it?" Allie asked.

Stephanie slumped in her chair. "I don't know," she wailed. "I have to think of something."

"Well, you don't have much time," Darcy told her. "Your date is tomorrow!"

"Whose date is tomorrow?"

The girls turned to see Stephanie's older sister, D.J., coming down the stairs. D.J. was eighteen and in college.

"My date," Stephanie answered. "But it's not a real date!"

D.J. stared at her younger sister. "Oh, one of those. Well, who's your unreal date with, then?" she asked.

"Michael Allen. A new guy," Stephanie told her.

"A new gorgeous guy," Darcy added.

16

"A new unbelievably gorgeous guy," Allie chimed in.

D.J. smiled. "Way to go, Steph! And where are you going with this gorgeous guy?" she asked.

Stephanie made a face. "We're not going anywhere. He's coming over here to see my video camera."

D.J. made a face back at Stephanie. "What's your problem?" she asked.

"Sorry, Deej," Stephanie said. "I'm just nervous about this whole thing. I kind of told Michael that Uncle Jesse's camera was mine and now he wants to come over and see it."

D.J. scowled. "Yikes, Steph. You know how protective Uncle Jesse is of his camera. He's never even let me hold it. He keeps it under lock and key."

Stephanie frowned. "Don't remind me," she groaned. "I never thought Michael would want to see it! What am I going to do?"

She fell back in her chair and laid her head on the table.

"Who cares what you do?" Darcy said. "He's coming over here. Michael Allen! The hottest guy in school is coming to your house. And every girl in the eighth grade is totally jealous!"

"How do you know that?" Stephanie asked.

"It's all over school!" Darcy explained. "Everyone's talking about the Big Date. Trust me, Steph. You and Michael are the hot topic on campus!"

Stephanie smiled and fell back into the chair again. "Really?" she asked. "Me? And Michael? As in, like, a couple?"

Darcy nodded. "Yup. Seems word about your date spread through the halls pretty fast."

"That's great, Steph," D.J. said. "So when's the big date?"

"What date?" Danny Tanner said, entering the kitchen.

"Oh, hi, Dad," Stephanie said, totally surprised. "Getting chilly out there, huh?" she said, trying to change the subject. She hadn't even heard him come in the front door, and the last thing she wanted was her father to think she had a big date. There'd be a hundred questions to answer, a list of dos and don'ts, and a curfew to start with.

"Did I hear someone say something about a date?" Danny said again as he put away the juice and wiped off the counter.

"No, Dad, you didn't. We were just talking about the due date of our assignment in media class, that's all," she said, glancing at Darcy and Allie.

"Yeah," D.J. said. "The media class with the real cute new boy who Stephanie doesn't have a date with."

"Stephanie," her dad said. "You can tell me if you have a date. That would be fine. I'll just have to meet him first, and then we'll discuss what time—"

"Dad, I swear I don't have a date," Stephanie said, gritting her teeth. "It's just a boy who's coming over tomorrow to talk about a media project."

"Oh, well, then that's okay," Danny said, picking up a sweater that was on the back of a chair and heading out of the kitchen.

Stephanie called after him, "Dad? Where are you going with that sweater?"

"I thought I'd toss it in the laundry," Danny answered.

"Dad," Stephanie said. "Get back here. That's Darcy's sweater you're about to wash."

Darcy, Allie, and D.J. broke into giggles as Danny apologized and put the sweater back on the chair. He was the resident neat freak, and nothing was safe from his "keep it clean" campaign.

"Allie, did you hear people talking about me

today?" Stephanie said when her father had left the kitchen.

Allie nodded. "All day," she said.

"Who?" Stephanie demanded. "Tell me who!"

"Those girls from our media skills class and then some kids at lunch."

"What did they say exactly?" Stephanie asked Allie. "Every word! Tell me!"

"One girl mentioned how you and Michael sat together and were already like best friends. I think another girl called you 'lucky.' "

Stephanie jumped up from her chair and clasped her hands together. "Lucky? They called me lucky! That's so cool!"

"Gee, Steph, get a grip, will ya? What's the big deal?" Darcy asked.

Stephanie put her hands on her hips and glared at Darcy. "The big deal," she said, "is that I, Stephanie Tanner, am dating the cutest guy in school!"

"I thought you said it wasn't a date," Allie reminded her.

"Well, it is a date. You heard him. He said, 'Don't forget about our date tomorrow,' right? So I guess it is a date after all."

Allie rolled her eyes. "Okay, Miss Popularity. And what are you going to do when your date asks to see the expensive video camera you bragged about?"

Allie and Darcy watched as their best friend slumped back into her chair one last time. "There's only one thing I can do," she groaned. "Beg Uncle Jesse to lend me his camera tomorrow afternoon."

# Chapter 3

Stephanie giggled when she pushed open the attic door and saw her aunt Becky and uncle Jesse. Jesse held four-year-old Nicky under one arm and Nicky's twin brother, Alex, under the other as Becky tickled their tummies.

"Stephie!" they cried. "Help! Help!"

Stephanie laughed and ran up to her uncle Jesse. "I know a secret about your daddy," she told the twins. "He's very ticklish under his chin!" She reached up to Jesse's face.

"You wouldn't!" Jesse warned her.

"Oh, wouldn't I?" Stephanie tickled as hard as she could.

Jesse burst out laughing and let go of the boys. "Okay! Okay!" he cried. "You win!"

Everyone fell to the floor, laughing. Then Jesse jumped up. "I have to get this on film!" he cried.

Becky groaned. "Jess, you're always filming us playing on the floor. Let's do something different. Maybe go outside or something."

Jesse unlocked the storage cabinet where he kept his camera. "What? Take the camera outdoors? It could rain! There could be a tornado and it could get swept away! An earthquake could—"

"Uh, Uncle Jesse," Stephanie interrupted, "does that camera have eight millimeters?"

Jesse stopped filming. "Well, as a matter of fact, it is an eight millimeter, Steph. How did you know that?"

*Yes!* Stephanie thought to herself. "Oh, just a guess," she replied, trying to sound casual.

Jesse pointed the camera at the twins. "Hey, come on, guys!" he said. "Do something cute!"

Alex and Nicky sat there silently, neither one of them moving an inch.

"Why is it that you two will never sit still or be quiet until I get this camera out?" Jesse said. "If it was time for bed, you'd be ready to sing and dance all night long."

Stephanie suddenly had an idea. If she could encourage the boys to sing on tape, her uncle might let her borrow his camera tomorrow as a way of thanking her. Might.

"I'll help you get the twinsters to sing," Stephanie said to Jesse. "But I need to ask a favor in exchange."

"If you can get these guys to sing into the camera, Stephanie, I will be eternally grateful. Anything you wish will be granted."

"Okay!" Stephanie said. She smiled at the twins. "Do you know 'B-I-N-G-O'?" She began. " 'There was a farmer had a dog—' "

" 'And Bingo was his name-o!' " the twins sang out. " 'B-I-N-G-O, B-I-N-G-O—' "

Aiming the camera at the twins, Jesse said, "Way to go, Steph! You did it."

"Now do I get my wish?" Stephanie asked hopefully.

But Jesse ignored her question and said, "We're on a roll. And it's time to rock."

"Uh-oh," Becky said. "I think I know what's next."

Jesse carefully handed the camera to Becky. "Okay, honey, now hold it gently."

Becky nodded. "I know, I know." She started taping the twins.

Jesse clapped his hands together. "Okay, guys! Forget about that stupid flea-bag mutt Bingo! Daddy's going to teach you an even better song about a dog."

Jesse plugged in his electric guitar, then ran his fingers through his thick black hair and curled his upper lip.

"Daddy, is this an Elvis song?" Alex asked, recognizing his father's impression immediately.

"Yes, it is, son," Jesse replied in his best Elvis voice. He strummed a loud electric guitar chord. He stared into the camera and started singing "Hound Dog."

Seconds later Nicky and Alex started jumping around him and singing too. Then they pulled Stephanie in front of the camera.

"Sing!" they ordered her.

Stephanie couldn't back out now. Soon the video camera would be in her hot little hands! She quickly grabbed a hairbrush for a microphone, curled her own lip, and began to rock and roll. She shook her long blond hair in front of her face and jumped around the room, hamming it up while her cousins giggled hysterically.

Comet, the Tanners' golden retriever, came up to see what all the commotion was about. Stephanie threw her arm around Comet and cuddled him, singing all the time.

Becky could barely hold the camera straight, she

was laughing so hard. Finally, Jesse hit the last chord and everyone fell in a heap on the floor.

"Daddy, why was that hound doggie crying all the time?" Nicky asked.

Jesse chuckled. "I'll tell you what," he said, "if you guys get to bed, I'll answer that question when I tuck you in."

Stephanie smiled as her cousins raced into their room. "Uh, Uncle Jess," she began, "about that favor—" She crossed her fingers behind her back.

"Sure," Jesse said. "But just a sec, I want to put the camera back where it belongs. Can't be too careful with this baby."

Stephanie noticed Becky roll her eyes. "We go through this every time," Becky whispered to her. "He's nuts."

Jesse unlocked the custom-made cabinet he had built especially to hold his camera. He put the camera gently into its case, then slid the case into the cabinet. Then he locked the cabinet door and put the key on top of the cabinet.

"Okay, Steph," he said with a smile. "What can I do for you?"

Stephanie was stunned at the fuss Jesse had made over the camera. *Becky was right. He was nuts.*

"Oh, well, it's nothing, really. You see, I have a

project for my media skills class to make a documentary."

Jesse's smile began to fade. "Go on," he said, rubbing his chin while he listened.

"Well," Stephanie hesitated, then continued. "I kind of need to, like, borrow your camera tomorrow, just to sort of, like, you know, show my friend."

"My camera?" Jesse asked in alarm.

"Well, yes. Your camera." Stephanie swallowed hard. There was no way her uncle would ever agree to this.

Jesse folded his arms across his chest and started pacing the attic apartment. Back and forth. Back and forth. Stephanie and Becky grew dizzy watching him.

"You promised if I got the twins to sing, that I could have anything I wanted," she reminded him.

"You did promise her," Becky joined in.

*Thank you, Becky,* Stephanie said silently. Then she said to Jesse, "Please, Jesse, please? I'll be extra careful! I promise!"

"Okay, okay," Jesse said. "You can use the camera."

"Bingo!" Stephanie cried out, jumping into the air.

"Under one condition," Jesse continued.

Stephanie's face fell.

"First thing Saturday morning I'll give you a lesson. Taking the Camera from Its Protective Case 101."

Stephanie was crushed. How could she tell Jesse she needed to have her hands on that camera tomorrow afternoon? And that she wanted to impress the new guy in school with it? Jesse would never understand.

Stephanie sighed and stared at the camera locked safely away in the cabinet.

*Time to move on to Plan B*, she thought.

Later that night Stephanie flopped onto her bed with a sigh. She groaned, "What am I going to wear tomorrow?"

Her younger sister, Michelle, sitting on her own bed across the room, asked, "What's wrong with the shirt you're wearing? I like that shirt."

Stephanie looked down at the white button-down ruffled shirt she wore and groaned. "It makes me look too . . . puffy," she replied.

"Can I have it, then?" Michelle asked eagerly.

Stephanie shrugged and tossed it to her. "I guess," she said.

"Cool! Thanks, Stephanie!"

Stephanie put on her bathrobe, then peered into

her closet and surveyed her new school outfits. "It's no use," she wailed. "I don't have anything cool to wear!" Nothing that would knock the socks off one Michael Allen.

Stephanie suddenly snapped her fingers in the air and dropped to her knees. Michelle stared at her in amazement as Stephanie buried herself deep in the huge pile of clothing and shoes at the bottom of her closet.

"Excellent!" Stephanie cried out in a muffled voice. When she emerged from the closet she held an old pair of faded jeans with huge tears at the knees. "I almost forgot about these! They're perfect!"

Michelle watched as her sister pulled on the jeans and buttoned them up. "Stephanie!" she said with a giggle. "You can't wear those, they're ripped! They have holes all over the place!"

Stephanie eyed her reflection in the full-length mirror and smiled. Sure, they had holes. That's why her dad had made her get rid of them. But holey jeans were a major fashion statement. That's why she'd secretly fished them out of the garbage and hid them away in her closet.

"Perfect!" she said again, staring at the gaping holes and the torn right cuff. It was exactly the look she was going for.

She tore off the jeans, pulled on her favorite black bodysuit, then put the jeans back on. She topped them off with an old flannel shirt, then checked it out in the mirror.

"Do I look grunge?" she asked Michelle.

Michelle wrinkled her nose. "You sure do. Very grungy."

"Good," Stephanie said. She glanced at Michelle and laughed. "Michelle, that shirt is a little big for you. You'll have to wait a few years before it fits."

Michelle looked down at the white blouse, which reached way below her knees and her hands. "Yeah, I guess you're right, Steph. But thanks for giving it to me anyway."

"No problem," Stephanie said. "But in exchange for the shirt you have to do me a favor." She paused. "I don't want Dad to see me in these jeans. He thinks I tossed them out months ago. You can't tell him that I'm wearing them tomorrow. Capiche?"

"Capiche?" Michelle repeated.

"It means 'Get it?' "

Michelle thought about it for a while. "Capiche," she replied.

# Chapter
# 4

♦ ◄ ♦ ♦

After homeroom Stephanie and Allie met in the hall and walked to their media skills classroom. Stephanie stopped short in the doorway and looked down at her jeans with the holes in them. "You don't think I look too put together, do you?" she asked nervously.

Allie laughed. "Put together?" she asked, staring at Stephanie's knee. "No, more like falling apart!"

"You know what I mean." Stephanie said. "I don't want Michael to think I dressed up for him."

"Dressed up?" Allie repeated.

"Allie!"

"Okay, okay! I know what you mean." She gave Stephanie a quick once-over. "No, you look fine. Terrific. Very funky."

Stephanie smiled. "Thanks," she said. "You're a pal." Then she pulled Allie into the classroom.

To her surprise, Michael was already in class. He was still as good-looking as she'd remembered. Maybe even better-looking.

"Hey, Michael," she said.

"Hi, Stephanie," he replied. "Great jeans!" he added with his lopsided smile. "Are we still going to your house after school?"

Stephanie nodded, but before she could speak, Mr. Merin called the class to order.

"I'm going to let you all get started on your projects today," Mr. Merin told them. "I've reserved space around the building for each group to meet in privacy. For the next two weeks you'll come in here for attendance, then split up and go to your designated meeting places."

Allie nudged Stephanie. "This class just gets better and better!" she whispered.

Stephanie's video group was assigned to work in the cafeteria. After Mr. Merin checked attendance, she, Allie, Michael, Karen Volpe, and Greg Washington packed up their bags and headed down the hall. The cafeteria was empty when they got there.

Stephanie suggested they sit at a table in the back. When they were all settled in, she opened her notebook and said, "I think we should first brainstorm and come up with a cool topic for our documentary."

"Good idea," Karen said.

Everyone agreed, then picked up their pens. It got quiet real fast.

Stephanie gazed around the table. "Doesn't anybody have ideas?" she asked.

No one said a word.

"Okay, well, that's what brainstorming is all about. Let's just throw out a bunch of topics—good or bad—and maybe we'll latch on to something that way."

Michael spoke first. "How about a video yearbook?" he suggested.

"Excellent!" Stephanie cried. "What an awesome idea! I vote for that. Let's do a video yearbook."

Karen shook her head. "How can we do a yearbook when the school year just started yesterday?" she asked. "No one's joined any clubs yet, and the football team and cheerleaders haven't even been picked."

"Good point," Greg said. "We can't do a yearbook."

Stephanie frowned. "I guess you're right," she said. Then she smiled at Michael. "But it was a good idea."

Michael grinned. "Thanks."

Allie raised her hand.

"You don't have to raise your hand, Allie," Stephanie told her. "We're not in class."

Allie turned red and lowered her hand. "Oh, right. It's just a habit, I guess."

"Do you have an idea?" Stephanie asked.

Allie nodded. "Sort of," she answered. "I was thinking, it would be really cool if we did it without a script and just filmed kids hanging out. Kind of like that show on MTV called *Real World*, where they just keep the camera rolling around these kids all the time and record everything they say."

Michael sat up in his seat and leaned forward. "Allie, that's a great idea! That show is awesome from a director's point of view. Very cutting-edge."

"Huh?" Greg asked.

Michael snickered. "Sorry, that's a Hollywood term. It means 'very now' and 'happening.' My uncle is a director, so I kind of picked up some of the language. Anyway, I think that's a great idea." He smiled at Allie. "Kind of like cinema verité."

"I know what that means," Stephanie jumped in. "My father and aunt are in the TV business, and they told me. It means a movie that's like real life."

"Well," she continued, "it *is* a good idea, Allie.

But we can't just go and film stuff with no story or anything."

"Okay, how about this?" Michael said. "What if we did a documentary about the different groups of kids here at school. You know, the jocks, the brains, the tough crowd, the . . . uh, does your school have a group of kids who think they're real popular?"

"The Flamingoes!" everyone answered at once.

"Okay, the Flamingoes, the school-spirit crowd, and then just the regular kids. Anyway, we can film the whole thing at lunch, here in the cafeteria, and just keep the camera on them, the way Allie suggested, and see what they talk about."

Stephanie nodded in excitement. "We can call it 'Doin' Lunch' or 'Cafeteria Bites' or something like that!" she announced.

Michael laughed. "That's pretty funny, Steph," he said. "Cafeteria Bites. I like that!"

Stephanie beamed. Michael thought she was funny!

"Me too," Greg said. "Did you just make that up?"

Stephanie nodded modestly. "Just now," she said.

"I think it's excellent," Karen said.

35

Allie smiled. "Stephanie's great at coming up with that kind of stuff."

"You're the creative type," Michael said. "I've got a lot of those kinds of people in my family. You know, Hollywood connections. Like my uncle," Michael went on. "Did I tell you he knows Arnold Schwarzenegger and Steven Spielberg?"

"Yes, you did," Stephanie said. "You told me that yesterday." Privately, Stephanie thought, this new guy may be cute, but he sure loves to talk about his "Hollywood connections."

"Oh," Michael said, and then paused. "I was thinking," he went on, "like maybe I should do all the filming for the movie. I mean, I've grown up with film people in the family, so maybe I should be the director too."

"You're going to be the director *and* the cameraman?" Stephanie asked. *Boy,* she thought to herself, *he sure does take charge.*

"Back in my old school," Michael explained, "I was the president of the video club. I directed movies all the time."

And Michael was amazingly confident, Stephanie thought, considering it was only his second day in a new school.

"It sounds like you have the most experience,"

Allie said. "Maybe he should be the director," she said to Stephanie.

"And the cameraman too?" Stephanie frowned.

"Does anyone else here know how to use a video camera?" Michael asked.

All five kids looked blankly at one another.

"It can't be all that hard to learn," Stephanie finally said. True, yesterday she hadn't known the difference between an eight-millimeter and a VHS, but if Michael could learn all about cameras, then why couldn't she? Maybe those lessons with Uncle Jesse weren't such a bad idea after all.

"Mr. Merin said there are two cameras that our class can use." Michael said. "But you guys have to figure out how to use them. In the meantime, I better start filming, or we're not going to have any footage by the time our project is due."

"I think you're right," Karen said. "I'll learn how to use one of the cameras this week."

"I'll use the other one," Greg volunteered.

"I'll be in charge of the narration," Stephanie said. "I'm a writer for the school newspaper," she explained to Michael. "I plan to be a journalist someday."

"I can be in charge of the sound track," Allie offered.

"Great," Michael said.

"I think we should have a really cool sound track," Stephanie said. "Like maybe we can pick ten songs from ten really cool groups."

"Excellent!" Michael exclaimed. "What about grunge music?"

"Allie is in charge of the sound track, remember?" Stephanie said to Michael. "Does the director get to do everything?"

"What about hip-hop?" Allie broke in.

"Boyz II Men," Greg suggested. "We should definitely have them in our sound track. They're hot."

"And Gloria Estefan," Karen added. "And R.E.M. too!"

"Sounds great!" Allie said. "I'll get to work on it right away."

"Let's also have the Spin Masters," Stephanie added, casting a glance at Michael. "They're excellent!" The Spin Masters were a really great band from New York who played music that was fun to dance to. She wanted him to know that she knew her grunge music.

Michael stared at her. "You like the Spin Masters?" he asked.

"Of course," she answered with a casual shrug.

"I love the Spin Masters," Michael said. "I saw them play in L.A. last year."

"Oh, yeah, me too," Stephanie lied.

Allie shot her a look.

"I mean, I saw them in San Francisco," she added. Well, she wasn't totally lying. She *had* seen the Spin Masters in San Francisco. What she didn't bother mentioning was the fact she'd seen their concert in her living room. On MTV.

"How'd you like the show?" Michael asked her.

Stephanie gulped. "Uh, it was hot," she answered. Just then Allie kicked her under the table. Stephanie felt bad for making up the story, but she couldn't help it. For some reason she felt she had to impress Michael—the same way he had tried to impress everybody with his uncle, the director.

"My uncle knows the Spin Masters, you know," she added.

Allie kicked her again.

"He does?" Michael asked.

Stephanie nodded, trying hard not to look in Allie's direction.

"What does your uncle do?" Greg asked.

"He's a rock star," Stephanie explained. "He's had an album out and toured and everything." She leaned back in her chair and casually crossed her legs, making sure they weren't in reach of Allie.

"Actually," she went on, "I was just jamming with my uncle Jesse last night. Nothing major, just a little Elvis tune."

Michael's mouth fell open. "Really?"

Stephanie nodded and examined her fingernails.

Greg and Karen waited eagerly for Stephanie to tell them more.

"Wait a sec!" Michael cried. "I have an excellent idea! Why don't you ask your uncle to get the Spin Masters to write a song for our movie?"

Greg nodded and turned to Stephanie. "Yeah! Can you?"

Stephanie nearly fell off her chair. "Huh?" she asked.

"It's a totally awesome idea," Michael went on. "It could be for the last scene. Imagine how cool that would be!"

"Yeah, cool," Stephanie croaked.

"Then you'll do it?" Michael asked. "You'll ask your uncle?"

"It would be fantastic," Karen said.

"Totally," Greg said. "Can you do it, Steph?"

Stephanie swallowed hard. Everyone was staring at her. *How am I going to get myself out of this one?* she thought frantically.

"Come on, Stephanie. What's it gonna be?" Michael asked.

"I don't know if—"

Michael didn't let her finish. "Since your uncle is such good friends with them, they'll probably do it," he decided. He pounded the table with both fists. "I'm psyched. Now, maybe it would be better if Allie handled the narrative and Stephanie handled the sound track. Is that all right with you two?" he asked, looking at Allie.

"But I thought I was the writer—" Stephanie began to say.

At the same time Allie shrugged and said, "It's okay with me."

"Then it's settled," Michael continued. "Stephanie, you'll handle the music. You've got the connections, right?"

Stephanie hesitated. All five kids were looking at her, waiting for an answer. "Right," she mumbled.

"And Allie will be the writer. This is so excellent, don't you think?" He smiled his adorable lopsided smile, but somehow Stephanie didn't think it was quite so adorable anymore.

"Yeah. Excellent," she muttered, trying her best to smile.

"So what did your uncle Jesse say about the camera?"

Allie and Stephanie had just joined Darcy in the cafeteria for lunch.

"Yeah," Allie said. "Did he say you could use it?"

"Well, sort of," Stephanie said, opening up her

carton of apple juice and avoiding her friends' questioning looks. *Why is it that ever since I met Michael Allen,* Stephanie thought, *my life has gotten extremely messy?*

"Your uncle Jesse said yes?" Darcy asked.

"Well, he said I could borrow it, but by the time I pass all his exams and fill out all the required paperwork, I'll be ninety-three."

"What are you talking about?" Darcy asked.

"It's a long story," Stephanie muttered.

"Well, what are you going to do?" Allie asked.

Stephanie put her elbows on the table and rested her chin in her palms. Sometimes she wished her friends didn't ask so many questions. "I did have one idea," she said, letting her voice trail off.

Darcy and Allie waited for her to finish. When she didn't, Darcy kicked the leg of her chair. "Are you going to tell us, or what?"

"Okay," Stephanie explained. "You see, Uncle Jesse and Aunt Becky won't be home until late this afternoon. Neither will my dad. And Joey is so busy with work, he'll be down in his office in the basement for most of the day. So I thought I'd sneak the camera out for when Michael shows up, then sneak it back."

Darcy and Allie exchanged glances.

"I'll stop off at the camera store on the way

home," Stephanie continued, "and buy a blank eight-millimeter cassette for me and Michael to use. When we're finished, I'll take it out, put Uncle Jesse's back in, and lock the camera back up, and he'll never know the difference!"

"Do you think you can get away with it?" Allie asked. "It sounds kind of dangerous."

"Won't Michael know something's wrong when you don't know how to use your uncle's camera?" Darcy pointed out.

Stephanie shook her head. "Nah, he's so excited to see an eight-millimeter camera up close, I'll just hand it right over to him and let him use it."

Allie stared at her friend. "That could work, you know."

Darcy nodded in agreement. "It just might," she said.

Stephanie sat back in her chair and let out a heavy sigh. "Let's hope so," she said.

"Boy, you were great at the video meeting today, Stephanie," Allie said. "You had really good ideas." She peeled open her sandwich and peeked at its contents. Then she closed it back up and took a bite.

"Oh, it was no big deal," Stephanie said. *Another one of my bright ideas has gotten me into big trouble,* she thought to herself.

"No big deal?" Allie said with a laugh. "You

were great! I wish I could do that. Come up with such fun ideas like that."

"Your ideas were good," Stephanie told her. "Michael seemed to think so too."

Allie blushed. "You don't mind that I'm going to write the narrative, do you?" Allie said.

"No, of course not," Stephanie answered.

"Good, 'cause now I have another question. How in the world are you going to get the Spin Masters to write a song for our video?"

"The Spin Masters?" Darcy asked.

Allie pointed to Stephanie. "Our best friend here told everyone in our video group that her uncle Jesse knows the Spin Masters and he'd ask them to write a song for our movie."

Darcy stared at Stephanie in amazement. "You did what?"

"Can we change the subject?" Stephanie said, too embarrassed to look up from her lunch. *How did I get myself into such a big mess?* she asked herself.

"Boy, Steph," Darcy said as if she could read her friend's mind, "you really got yourself into a big mess this time."

"Thanks for pointing that out to me," Stephanie said.

"What are friends for?" Darcy said.

# Chapter
# 5

◆  ◀  ◾  ◆

Stephanie watched impatiently as Joey put the finishing touches on his waffles. First he smeared butter across the steaming hot waffles, then he slowly poured maple syrup into each individual waffle hole.

Stephanie thought she would lose her mind.

She glanced at the clock over the kitchen sink, then bit her thumbnail. Michael was going to be ringing her doorbell any minute. She had to get Joey back downstairs before Michael arrived. She didn't want Michael to meet anyone in her family. He might say something about the video camera being hers. Or even something about the song she'd promised the Spin Masters would do.

Joey opened the fridge and stared inside.

"What are you looking for now?" Stephanie asked anxiously.

"Blueberries," Joey answered. "I thought there were some left over. Boy, they would really go great on top of my waffles." He continued searching the shelves in the fridge.

Stephanie rolled her eyes and checked the clock again. "Uh, Joey, don't you have a load of work to do today?"

"Sure do, Steph," Joey replied. "That's why I'm making this little snack here. Food helps me think. Ah-ha! Here they are!"

Excellent, Stephanie thought. *Now he'll go downstairs and give me a chance to run up and get the camera.*

"Awesome snack. Better eat it before it gets cold and mushy."

Joey lifted the plate of waffles, licked his lips, then headed for the basement door. He was just about to turn the knob, when he snapped his fingers and spun around.

"Bananas!" he cried.

"Bananas?" Stephanie asked.

"I can't eat these waffles without bananas!"

Stephanie held her breath and watched the clock as Joey peeled a banana and cut it into slices. Then he dropped the slices one by one on top of his waffles. When he was finally finished, Stephanie ran to the basement door and held it open for him.

"*Bon appétit!*" she said with a smile.

Joey smiled back and started down the stairs. He'd walked only three steps, when he turned and snapped his fingers again.

"Walnuts!" he cried.

Stephanie had to think fast. "I ate them!" she lied. "This morning. For breakfast."

"The entire bag?" Joey asked.

"Yup!" Stephanie replied. "You know me. A real walnut freak. Can't get enough of 'em!"

Joey's shoulders drooped in disappointment, and he continued down the stairs.

Stephanie closed the basement door behind him, then raced upstairs to her uncle's attic apartment. She had only a few minutes to find the key, unlock the cabinet, and bring the camera downstairs. When Stephanie entered the attic apartment she went directly to the camera cabinet. The key wasn't on top!

*Okay, try not to panic*, she told herself. *If I were Uncle Jesse, where would I put the key?*

She checked the desk drawer, but it wasn't there. She checked the guitar case too, but no luck. Then she glanced up at the framed photograph hanging on the wall next to the cabinet. It was a photo of

Uncle Jesse and Aunt Becky at Graceland—Elvis Presley's Tennessee home.

"Of course!" she cried. She reached up and felt along the top of the frame. The key slid off and fell to the floor.

"Bingo!" she exclaimed. "B-I-N-G-O!"

Stephanie opened the cabinet and pulled the camera from its case. She put the case back in the cabinet, then ran back downstairs, where she'd left the blank cassette. She was just about to pop the cassette into the camera, when the doorbell chimed. She placed the camera and cassette down on the coffee table, checked herself out in the hall mirror, then opened the door.

"Hi, Michael," she said, still a little out of breath. The first thing that Stephanie noticed was that Michael was wearing sunglasses. On a cloudy day. He also wore his black leather jacket and carried a backpack.

"Hey!" Michael replied.

"So, come on in," Stephanie said, checking out his Ray-Bans.

Stephanie suddenly realized she was a little nervous. She'd been so busy worrying about sneaking Uncle Jesse's camera out and switching tapes and everything, she hadn't really thought about the fact that she'd have to spend time with Michael in her house. And she hardly knew him.

"Well, this is where I live," she mumbled with a shrug.

Michael laughed. "I figured," he said.

"Right." Stephanie felt her face get hot. She didn't really know what to talk about. Michael always acted so cool. Like now. He still had his sunglasses on. Maybe he'd just forgotten he was wearing them. They were cool enough outside—but wearing sunglasses inside was more weird than cool.

"Uh, why don't you sit down," she suggested. "Are you hungry?"

Michael shook his head. "No. So where's your camera?"

"Right here," she said, pointing to the coffee table. He probably can't see anything with the dark glasses on, she thought to herself. Should I remind him he's wearing them? Flustered, Stephanie picked up Uncle Jesse's camera and handed it to Michael.

"Wow!" Michael said as he took the camera. "This is just like my uncle Mario's camera. Can I turn it on?"

"Oh, sure," Stephanie said, glancing around. She

prayed Joey wouldn't decide to come upstairs for more waffles.

Michael turned the camera on and pointed it at Stephanie. "So, Stephanie Tanner," he said, "which school clique do you belong to? The jocks? The brains?"

Stephanie blushed. "Are you filming this?" she asked.

"Yup."

"Oh, well, in that case," she said, striking a silly pose, "I'm part of the popular clique!" She flashed a smile at the camera and batted her eyelashes.

Michael laughed. "And tell me, O Popular One. Who do you sit with in the cafeteria?"

Stephanie thought for a moment, then struck another pose. "With the popular kids, of course!" she said.

Michael laughed again.

"Actually," Stephanie said more seriously, "I'm not so popular. I'm just a regular kid. Part of the regular-kid crowd, I guess."

"And what about Allie?" Michael asked.

Why did he want to know about Allie? Stephanie wondered. "Allie Taylor?" Stephanie asked, knowing fully well who Michael meant.

Michael nodded.

"Yes, um, I sit with Allie. She's my best friend."

With the camera pointed at her, Stephanie didn't know what to do with her hands, so she stuck them into her pockets.

"So who do you have for history?" Michael asked, suddenly switching topics.

Stephanie thought it was strange. "Ms. Shapot," she answered. "Why?"

"Do you like her?" Michael asked.

Stephanie shrugged. "I guess. I don't know. She's kind of boring." When she said "boring," she rolled her eyes and sneered. It made Michael chuckle, so she did it again.

Michael kept filming. "So how long have you and Allie been friends?"

Stephanie made a face. Back to Allie again. Weird. She wondered why Michael asked so many questions about her.

"Uh, since kindergarten," she answered. "We've gone to school together every year."

"Tell me something about you and Allie that nobody else knows," Michael asked her.

"What do you mean?" Stephanie asked, thinking that Michael was kind of nosy.

"You know, tell me a secret about you and Allie."

Stephanie didn't know what to say. She barely knew this guy, and he was asking her such weird questions. She was beginning to feel uneasy. Tell him something safe, she told herself.

"Well, Allie, Darcy, and I meet at the pay phone by the girls' gym every morning before class. We've been doing it every day since sixth grade. Nobody else really knows that."

"Cool. Is that it?"

Stephanie nodded. "Can you turn the camera off now?" she asked.

Michael looked up from the camera. "Sure, Stephanie. Is something wrong?"

"Uh, no. It's just that I'm kind of hungry. Want to go to the kitchen?"

"I guess." He turned the camera off and slipped it back into the case.

Stephanie pulled out the cassette and handed it to Michael. "I'm going to, uh, put the camera away now. Keep it away from my little sister and my nephews. You know what I mean." She smiled awkwardly, then ran up the stairs.

When she came back down, Michael was waiting for her in the kitchen. With Joey.

Her heart skipped a beat. "Oh, hi, Joey!" she said. She wondered what they'd talked about while she was upstairs.

"Hey, Steph," Joey said. "I met your friend Michael here."

Stephanie managed to smile.

"So, Michael," Joey continued. "What's with the shades? If you want, I can lend you some sunscreen. I've got some SPF three hundred twenty-seven, which should block out all the ultraviolet rays in this kitchen."

"Huh?" Michael asked. "Oh, these," he said, removing the sunglasses.

*Finally*, Stephanie thought, trying to hide her smile.

"Stephanie," Michael said, "you didn't tell me Joey is the same Joey from that morning radio show. I listen to Joey and Jesse every morning!"

"Aw, go on," Joey said modestly.

"No, really," Michael told him. "You guys crack me up! I loved that bit you did about Popeye and Olive Oyl on *Love Connection.*"

Stephanie smiled and put her arm around Joey. "Yup, that's our very own Joey Gladstone. Radio star. And he was just leaving, weren't you, Joey?" She winked at Joey, hoping he'd take the hint. She didn't want Michael to mention the camera.

"As a matter of fact, I was just leaving," he said, winking back uneasily at Stephanie. "I have to get back downstairs. Work on . . . some radio stuff. Nice meeting you, Michael."

"Same here," Michael said.

Stephanie breathed a sigh of relief after Joey left. *That was close*, she thought.

Stephanie found a box of doughnuts in the fridge and tossed them on the table. "Here. Help yourself."

"You were the hungry one, remember?"

"Oh, right." Stephanie reached into the box and pulled out a jelly doughnut. She hated jelly doughnuts, but she ate it anyway.

Michael fished out a chocolate doughnut and took a bite. "You didn't tell me your whole family was famous," he said.

Stephanie nodded eagerly. "Oh, sure. Joey is a famous comedian. And my dad and my aunt Becky host a TV show called *Wake Up San Francisco*. They're pretty famous too. In San Francisco at least."

"I've seen that show!" Michael exclaimed. "That's your dad?"

Stephanie nodded. "And Jesse, from Joey and Jesse on *Rush Hour Renegades*, is my uncle."

"The musician?"

"Uh-huh."

"Stephanie, your family is so cool!" Michael seemed really impressed. "So, has your uncle talked to Chris Barton yet?"

Stephanie swallowed loudly. "Who?" she asked.

"Chris Barton. The lead singer of the Spin Masters."

"Right. I knew that. Uh, no, he hasn't had a chance. I think they're on tour or something. Maybe in Australia. Very busy," she lied.

"That's weird," Michael said. "I just heard they were playing a concert in San Francisco this weekend. Out at Golden Gate Park."

Stephanie froze. Uh-oh. "Really?" she asked. "Well, I guess that's why he hasn't been able to get in touch with them. They must be busy rehearsing."

"Must be," Michael said. "So, guess who's going to be at my uncle's wedding this Sunday?"

"Who?" Stephanie asked.

"Steven Spielberg!" Michael said excitedly. "Isn't that so cool? And I think some other stars will be there too. Like Tom Cruise."

"Really?" Stephanie asked.

"I've met Steve before, you know," Michael said, cutting her off. "Steve Spielberg. Lots of times."

*Did he just say "Steve" Spielberg?* she wondered.

"Yeah, should be fun," Michael went on. "I was thinking of asking him some pointers about movie making—you know, cinematography, to help with the documentary. I have some great ideas for it."

"That's a good idea," Stephanie said. "Maybe you can—"

"When I was the president of the video club in my old school, I directed movies all the time. All of them were excellent."

Stephanie nodded and smiled, but she couldn't help thinking that Michael sounded kind of conceited.

"For our movie I want to try and get some kids in the lunchroom to talk about their classmates," he added. "Get them to say really personal things about one another. Or maybe film them without them knowing."

"You mean spy on them?" Stephanie asked.

"Not really," Michael replied. "My uncle always says that people are more themselves if they don't know there's a camera on them. Once they see a camera, everyone turns into a big phony."

Stephanie stared at Michael. "I don't agree—"

"Anyway, I have some other cool ideas too, but I guess I'll tell you them tomorrow. At the meeting."

Stephanie nodded awkwardly. Michael thought all his ideas were cool. And he barely let her get a word in edgewise. That made her especially crazy.

Stephanie glanced up and gasped when she noticed the time. Her father would be home soon. She didn't want him to know the reason Michael was there—to look at the camera. Not to mention the fact she was wearing the jeans she'd promised to destroy.

"What is it?" Michael asked.

"Oh, nothing, really. I, uh, just remembered something. My, uh, library book. It's due today. I'm going to have to ask Joey to take me there so I can return it."

"Now?" Michael asked.

"Uh-huh," Stephanie nodded. "Right now. So I guess I'll see you tomorrow. In class."

Michael stared at her strangely, then got up from the table. He popped the rest of the doughnut into his mouth, then went into the living room for his backpack. Putting his sunglasses back on, he said, "So I'll see you," he said. "Tomorrow in class."

"Yup. In class," Stephanie said, ushering him out the door. She waved as Michael walked to the sidewalk. Then she closed the door behind him and breathed a huge sigh of relief. *Everybody in school thinks he's so cool*, she thought, rolling her eyes. *But maybe he's just a little too cool for me.*

She was still standing with her back against the door when her father came in from the kitchen carrying a handful of mail. Michelle was right behind him.

"Dad!" Stephanie exclaimed as Michelle ran past her and up to her room.

"Hi, sweetheart," Danny Tanner greeted his daughter. "Who was that?"

"Who was what, Dad?" Stephanie asked innocently.

"I heard you talking to someone in here," Danny said.

Stephanie laughed. "Oh, that? That was just a guy I know from school. Michael. We're doing a project together for media skills."

"Oh, that's nice," Danny said, taking a seat on the sofa. He continued sorting through the mail.

Stephanie glanced at the stairs a few feet away. She wondered if she could make it upstairs without her father noticing her clothes.

Taking a deep breath, Stephanie made a mad dash for the stairs. She was halfway up when her father called her name.

"Stephanie?"

Stephanie stopped. "Yes, Dad?"

"Leave those jeans on your bed after you take them off, please. I'll throw them out personally tomorrow morning."

Stephanie gulped. "Yes, Dad," she said.

When Stephanie got upstairs she found Michelle playing with her stuffed animals. About twelve of them were sitting in rows on her bed. And on Stephanie's bed Michelle was parading a big fuzzy panda from one end to the other.

Stephanie took her torn jeans off and slipped on

a pair of sweat pants. She had planned to stretch out on her bed and relax, but Michelle apparently had other ideas.

"Michelle?"

"What, Stephanie?"

"What exactly are you doing on my bed anyway?"

"It's a fashion show," Michelle explained. "Peaches the Panda is modeling the latest fall looks."

"And whose shirt is Peaches the Panda wearing?" Stephanie continued.

"My shirt," Michelle answered. "Don't you remember? You gave it to me last night."

Stephanie looked at the ruffled white shirt she'd given to Michelle. It was a nice shirt, and she'd wondered why she hadn't liked it yesterday, though she had to admit it fit Peaches the Panda perfectly. Then she looked down at the ripped jeans her father wanted to throw out—her favorite soft, faded, holey jeans.

With a sigh Stephanie said, "This wasn't one of my better days."

# Chapter

# 6

◆ ◀ ▪ ◆

"I wanted to call you last night, but D.J. had the phone tied up all night gabbing to her friend Kimmy," Stephanie explained to Darcy and Allie as they made their way to lunch. They'd all gotten to school late that morning and hadn't had a chance to talk.

"So how did the big date go?" Darcy asked.

"Once and for all, it wasn't a big date, I assure you," Stephanie said.

"What happened? Tell us everything," Allie prodded as they stood in the cafeteria line.

"Well, you wouldn't believe what Michael was wearing when he showed up. Sunglasses and a leather jacket."

"So?" Allie said. "What's so weird about that?"

"Well, I mean, he kept the sunglasses on in the house. And then he started talking about 'Steve' Spielberg."

"I can't believe he actually knows Steven Spielberg," Darcy said with wide eyes.

"Yeah, he keeps reminding me every chance he gets," Stephanie said.

"I'd like to meet Steven Spielberg," Allie said. "So then what happened, Stephanie?"

"Well, nothing much," Stephanie said. "He interviewed me on camera for a while. That's all. It's just that he acts so cool all the time."

"I thought you said he was the most gorgeous guy you'd ever seen," Darcy said to Stephanie. "Don't you think he is anymore?"

"Well, yeah, he's good-looking," Stephanie said. "But looks aren't everything."

"And at least he knows something about cameras," Allie added. "I don't know how we'd do this media project without him. Speaking of the media project, Steph, have you figured out what you're going to do about the Spin Masters song? What did you tell Michael yesterday?"

Stephanie opened her mouth to answer, then shut it. She hadn't quite figured out how to get out of that mess, and was hoping maybe Jesse could help her out. If the Spin Masters really were in town, who knows? Maybe Jesse could ask them to write the song. It was worth a shot.

"Actually, Darcy—" Stephanie started to say. Just then she saw a group of kids approaching them and stopped talking. Stephanie couldn't believe her eyes. Michael was coming toward them, his camera up to his eye. At least five kids were walking with them, and they were talking and laughing. "Oh, hi, Stephanie!" Susan Dunbar called out. "Look! Michael is filming us!"

"We're movie stars!" Cindi Wang said.

"Hi, guys. Hi, Michael," Stephanie said.

Michael lowered the camera. "Hey, Steph. I thought I'd start interviewing kids on the way to lunch. You know, get as much footage as possible so we had lots of film to edit."

Stephanie nodded. "Good idea, Michael. So, uh, do you want to interview Darcy and Allie?"

Michael smiled. "Definitely," he said, winking at Stephanie.

During their media class, she Allie, and Michael had decided to work on their project during lunch. As Michael interviewed Darcy and Allie, the crowd around them grew larger, and soon Stephanie couldn't hear the questions Michael asked, or how her friends answered.

After he interviewed Allie and Darcy, they all headed over toward the cheerleaders' table.

"Let me talk to them," Stephanie said to Michael. "I'll tell them they're going to be movie stars or something. I'm sure they'll let us film."

Stephanie approached Courtney Elliott, one of the cheerleaders. Stephanie knew Courtney pretty well—they'd been in the same French class two years in a row.

"Hi, Courtney! Can I ask you a question?"

"Hey, Stephanie! What's up?" Courtney had been a cheerleader since sixth grade.

"We're making a movie for media skills," Stephanie told her. "About the cafeteria. Do you guys want to be in it?"

Courtney smiled. "Sure! That would be so cool! We've already heard all about it."

Courtney's fellow cheerleaders seemed pretty excited too, but Stephanie thought they seemed more interested in Michael than in being in the movie.

"Is he your boyfriend?" Courtney whispered to Stephanie.

"Uh, not really," Stephanie told her.

"Too bad," Courtney said. "He's hot!"

Stephanie leaned closer to Courtney and whispered in her ear. "Well, we did have this one sort of date," she said.

"Really?" Courtney asked. "You went out with him?"

Stephanie opened her mouth to answer, but suddenly Michael was pointing his camera in their faces.

"And what are you two talking about?" he asked.

"Uh, nothing!" Stephanie said. "We were, uh, just getting ready. Are you ready?" she asked Courtney.

Courtney nodded.

Michael began filming and Stephanie immediately realized how all the cheerleaders turned on the phony charm.

"It must be so cool to be a director!" one girl said, flirting with Michael.

Michael laughed. "Just pretend I'm not here," he said. "Act natural."

"My cousin is in film school," another girl said, trying to impress him.

Stephanie rolled her eyes. Everyone was trying to get Michael's attention. *Pathetic!* she thought to herself.

"My mother met Demi Moore once," someone said.

*Hey, wait a minute. I know that voice!* Stephanie spun around.

"Darcy!"

"Well, she did!" Darcy said. "She met her at a restaurant last year in Seattle."

Stephanie rolled her eyes again.

"Hey, I have backstage passes to a Janet Jackson concert next week," a tall redheaded girl announced.

Michael spun around to get her on film. "I met her," he said.

"Who? Janet Jackson?" the girl asked.

"Yup," Michael replied, not looking up from the camera. "My uncle worked on one of her music videos once."

All the cheerleaders stared at Michael.

"Wow," Courtney said. "And he introduced you to her?"

Michael kept the camera rolling. "Uh-huh. I've met lots of famous people."

Stephanie watched as all the girls hung on Michael's every word. "My uncle Jesse introduced me to the Beach Boys and—" Stephanie began to say. But no one heard her. They all had their eyes glued to Michael.

"What was Janet Jackson like?" one girls asked Michael.

"She was really nice," Michael said. "We had a long talk about music."

"Well, my uncle almost opened for the Rolling Stones," Stephanie blurted out.

Everyone turned toward her.

"It, uh, fell through though," she added. "But he did get to meet them."

"Stephanie's uncle knows the Spin Masters," Michael told everyone. "And he's getting them to write a song for this movie!"

All the girls looked at Stephanie.

"Really?" Courtney asked.

"Um—" Stephanie didn't know what to say. Somehow she had to get out of her promise. But then Michael pointed the camera in her face. She was trapped.

"*Are* you going to get the Spin Masters to write a song for you?" Courtney asked.

It got uncomfortably quiet and Stephanie felt all eyes on her. Michael stepped in closer and stuck the camera about three inches from her face. She cast a sideways glance at Allie and Darcy, who were waiting for her answer.

Stephanie smiled into the camera and ran her fingers through her hair. "Sure, no problem. I'll get the song."

Michael smiled, then went back to filming. "Cool," he said with a grin.

The other girls stared enviously at Stephanie.

"Wow, you're so lucky!" Courtney whispered to her.

Stephanie smiled at her. *Lucky*, she thought as an enormous knot formed in the pit of her stomach. She'd better be lucky! Because somehow, somewhere, she had to be lucky enough to find a very special song.

# Chapter
# 7

◆ ◀ ▪ ◆

"I can't believe that Michael Allen," Stephanie said. "Bragging that he's met Janet Jackson. Right. Like I really believe that."

"Yeah, some people are the biggest liars!" Allie said, nudging Darcy. "*Some* people say they've got connections with people they don't even know."

Stephanie knew Allie was talking about her, so she changed the subject. "I don't know how you talked me into this meeting!" She tossed a batch of paper plates onto the kitchen table.

"You didn't have a choice," Allie reminded her. She straightened the plates and put out six paper cups at each setting. "The video group has to meet here. You live closest to school!"

Stephanie groaned. "Well, what am I going to

do if Uncle Jesse comes home when Michael is here? He might bring up the video camera, or the Spin Masters."

Darcy snickered. "You should have thought of that before you opened your mouth."

Stephanie glared at her. "I thought you were here to help out!" she yelled.

"I'm sorry," Darcy said. "But you have to admit, this whole thing is pretty funny."

Stephanie glared at her and she stopped talking. "It isn't funny, Darcy. The whole thing is pathetic!" she wailed. "If Michael finds out I lied, my whole life will be ruined!"

"Oh, Stephanie," Allie joked, "not your whole life! Just your reputation at school."

"Whose side are you on anyway?" Stephanie asked.

Allie giggled. "I'm on your side. You know that. We'll have our meeting, then Michael will go home. Chances are he'll never even see your uncle."

"But what if he does?" Stephanie worried.

"We'll think of something," Darcy assured her. "It's not like you've never been in this kind of trouble before."

"Yeah," Allie agreed. "It's almost like that time

you promised to get your uncle Jesse to play for our class carnival. And he said no."

"Somehow, that doesn't make me feel better," Stephanie pointed out.

"Yeah, but he ended up playing at the carnival anyway, and your reputation was saved." Darcy smiled brightly. "See? You always work something out. Just don't worry!"

Stephanie was still worrying when the front doorbell rang. She let Michael, Karen, and Greg in and showed them to the kitchen.

"Stephanie," Michael said, opening his backpack, "this cassette we used the other day has a bunch of stuff on it of your family."

Stephanie gasped in horror. "No way!"

Michael nodded. "Yeah, it's like a home movie. So I used my dad's equipment to record your interview onto another tape. Here, you can have this back."

Stephanie's face turned bright red. She snatched the cassette from Michael and ran up to the attic apartment. Luckily, Jesse and Becky weren't home yet. Stephanie quickly put the cassette back in the camera. *That was way too close!* she thought. In the kitchen Stephanie listened to Michael talk about the footage he'd shot that day, but she could barely keep still. She was too nervous that her uncle Jesse would walk in at any moment and everything would be ruined.

"So, Stephanie, when do you think we'll have that song from the Spin Masters?" Michael asked. "Our project's due next Friday."

Stephanie bit her bottom lip. "Don't worry," she snapped at him. "You'll have it!"

"This is going to be so cool!" Greg said. "The Spin Masters! Wow!"

Stephanie wished he'd shut up.

"Do we have a back-up plan?" Allie suddenly asked. "I mean, in case, for some reason, the Spin Masters can't write a song for us?"

"If Stephanie says they'll do it," Michael told her, "they'll do it. Right, Stephanie?"

Stephanie smiled nervously. "Right," she managed to say.

"But when?" Karen asked. "This project is due soon and—"

"Tonight!" Stephanie blurted out. "He'll talk to them tonight, okay?" Without turning around, she could tell Allie and Darcy were staring at her. She ignored them.

"Did you get some good stuff yesterday afternoon at lunch?" she asked Michael.

"Great stuff!" Michael exclaimed. "Let me show

you guys the dailies," he added, getting up from his chair.

"The what?" Karen asked.

Michael snickered. "Oh, sorry about that. Another Hollywood term. The dailies is the daily footage I shoot."

Everyone followed Michael into the living room. Stephanie couldn't believe how conceited Michael sounded. She wondered if the others had noticed.

Michael popped the tape in the VCR and pressed play. Almost immediately Courtney Elliott's face appeared on screen. The scene from when they interviewed the cheerleaders unfolded before their eyes. They had all been at the actual interview, but somehow, watching it on TV, it seemed different.

"Michael," Allie exclaimed, "this is great!"

"Terrific," Darcy added.

Karen and Greg agreed. "You're really good at this stuff," Greg said.

Stephanie watched the cheerleader piece in amazement. It really was good. The camera angles were great, and Michael asked really fun questions. And the way he had edited it, the scene didn't even seem like the same interview Stephanie had watched the previous day.

"We love being cheerleaders," Courtney Elliott

was saying. "We're like one big, happy family. We tell each other everything."

"I can't stand her," another girl said in the following scene, pointing at Courtney. "She's such a know-it-all."

Stephanie gasped. "When did that girl say that about Courtney?" she asked. "I don't remember that."

Michael grinned. "That's because you aren't the director. A good director knows where to look. Where to get the real story."

Stephanie's eyes narrowed. "Well, you can't leave that in," she said. "It's totally mean!"

"Shhh!" Karen said. "Check this out!"

They all turned back and watched as Courtney spoke seriously into the camera. "These are my best friends," she said about the other cheerleaders. "They're like sisters to me. And Stephanie, well, we're close too. Even if she isn't on the squad. She's a wonderful person."

Stephanie was about to smile, when the scene on-screen quickly changed. She suddenly saw her very own face on TV, her eyes rolling at what Courtney had just said.

"Hey!" Stephanie said, jumping up from the sofa. "I didn't do that at her! You made it seem as if I was making fun of her!"

Everyone stared at Stephanie.

"Tell them, Michael. I wasn't rolling my eyes at Courtney. I was talking about my history teacher when I rolled my eyes. That was the day you came over and interviewed me here at the house. You edited it like that on purpose! Tell them! I would never do that to a friend!"

Before Michael could answer, the scene changed again and suddenly Allie and Darcy appeared on-screen. They were both laughing.

"We're the nerds!" Darcy screamed into the camera.

Allie cracked up. "The biggest nerds in school!"

"No, actually, we're just regular kids. A little clique without a name. Just me, Allie, and Stephanie."

"Stephanie's the best!" Allie said. "There isn't a better friend than Stephanie Tanner!"

Stephanie turned to smile at Allie, when she suddenly saw herself on-screen again.

"Allie Taylor?" she watched herself say. "She's kind of boring." The Stephanie on-screen rolled her eyes and made a face.

Stephanie leapt up and snapped off the VCR. "Michael! How could you do that?"

Allie stood and faced Stephanie. "Stephanie, why did you say that about me?"

"Allie, I didn't! I was talking about Ms. Shapot. You know how boring she can be. Michael edited it so that it would look like I was talking to you. Right, Michael?"

"Totally right, Stephanie," Michael said. "Allie, we were just joking around, I promise. I edited that last night with my dad's equipment at home. I wanted to show you how things can be edited out of context to make them more . . . interesting."

Allie stared at them. "Well, that certainly was interesting."

"Allie, I swear! I didn't say that! Don't be mad, please?" Stephanie begged.

"I'm not mad, I guess," Allie said. "I'm just not sure I like this kind of movie."

"Me either," Stephanie said. "I think we need to have another brainstorming meeting and come up with a different movie idea. One that won't start a world war or anything!"

Michael stared innocently at Stephanie. "Why?" he asked. "If everyone knows it's only a joke, then what's the big deal?"

Karen shook her head. "Stephanie is right, Michael. People might get upset."

Michael sighed. "Okay. I'll take out the parts you want me to. But I still think the Cafeteria Bites idea is good. We should keep that."

Stephanie looked at the others. "That's okay

with me," she said. "But let's take a vote. All in favor of Cafeteria Bites, raise your hands."

All hands went up.

"And all in favor of cutting out the mean parts," Stephanie added, "raise your hands."

Again, all hands went up.

Stephanie shrugged. "So that's that," she said. "It's been decided. End of meeting."

"But we haven't talked about when we'll film our next segment, or who it's going to be," Greg pointed out.

Stephanie glanced at her watch. "We'll do it tomorrow," she snapped at him.

Greg made a face, and Stephanie felt bad for snapping at him. "I'm sorry, Greg," she said, softening. "I'm just really stressed out about this math test I have tomorrow. I really have to start studying."

"No problem," Greg said. "So let's just meet in class tomorrow."

"Sounds good," Michael said, packing up his equipment. "And then you can tell us about your uncle's conversation with the Spin Masters."

Stephanie gulped and nodded. "Right," she said, ushering them all out the door. She glanced hopelessly at Allie and Darcy before shutting the door behind them.

As she leaned against the door, Stephanie caught sight of her reflection in the hall mirror. She leaned forward and studied her face from all angles.

"I wonder," she said out loud, pulling on her chin, "how someone with such a small face could have such a big mouth."

Stephanie sat on the sofa after dinner, staring at the TV but not really watching the show, when Uncle Jesse came bursting through the front door.

"Guess what, Steph?" he cried happily. "I got the gig!"

Stephanie turned down the volume. "Great, Uncle Jesse! What gig?"

"Only the hottest gig in town!" he exclaimed, flopping down on the sofa. He put his legs up on the coffee table, leaned back, and folded his arms cross his chest.

"Your very own uncle," he announced, "the uncle who is sitting next to you at this very minute, has nabbed the biggest opening spot in the country for Friday night!"

Stephanie smiled. "Who are you opening for?" she asked.

"The Spin Masters!" Jesse cried. "Can you believe it?" He put up his hand for Stephanie to slap in a high-five, but Stephanie just stared at him, gaping in surprise.

"No way!" she said.

"Way, way, way!" Jesse exclaimed.

Stephanie gave him a super-duper high five. "Uncle Jesse, that's excellent! You have no idea how excellent that really is," she added. *Maybe this whole thing will work out after all*, she hoped.

"You're telling me," Jesse said. "My band beat out five other bands for the spot!"

Stephanie fell back on the sofa and stared at him in shock. This was way too good to be true. In fact, it was perfect! Now Uncle Jesse really could ask the Spin Masters to write a song for the documentary!

"Uncle Jesse," she said, "will you get to meet the Spin Masters?"

Jesse nodded. "Yeah, sure. We're rehearsing together tomorrow afternoon. I haven't told you the best part," he added. "We'll be doing a song with them!"

Stephanie's eyes widened. It was like a dream come true.

"There's more," Jesse said with a twinkle in his eye. Stephanie looked at him curiously. How could he top meeting and singing with the Spin Masters?

Jesse stood up, reached into his back pocket, and removed something. Something small and flat, with print on it. Something that looked an awful lot like—

"Tickets? For me?" Stephanie cried out.

"Better than that!"

Stephanie just stared at Jesse, awestruck. Her eyes widened and she said, "No!"

"Yes!" Jesse said. "Two backstage passes for you and your favorite person. One more for Becky. Now, what more could you possibly ask of me?"

Stephanie couldn't believe her luck. But there was still that little matter of the song. "Ummm, Uncle Jesse," Stephanie said slowly. "Actually there is one small thing I'd like to ask you."

"Shoot," Jesse said. "But make it quick. I have to meet with the band and go over our song list."

"Sure. It's, well, more like a favor."

Jesse's eyes narrowed. "Does it have to do with my camera?" he asked.

"No," Stephanie replied. "It has to do with the Spin Masters."

Jesse sat back down. "What is it?" he asked.

Stephanie took a deep breath. "Do you think, if you asked the Spin Masters to write a song for our documentary, they would?"

Jesse started laughing. "You're kidding, right?"

Stephanie laughed too. Then she abruptly stopped and said, "No. I'm serious."

Jesse stopped laughing. "Stephanie! The Spin Masters aren't going to just stop everything they're doing and write a song for a bunch of kids they don't even know!"

"Well, they might!" Stephanie protested.

"Stephanie, that's crazy! How can you even ask something like that?"

Stephanie slumped into the sofa cushions. It was a full thirty seconds before she spoke.

"I guess I *am* crazy," she finally said. "You see, I kind of told the kids at school that you were this big rock and roll star and—"

"Yeah? So? What's the problem?"

"I'm getting to it," she said. "So I told them you knew the Spin Masters and you would ask them to write a song for our documentary sound track."

"You what?" Jesse asked in shock.

"I know, I know!" Stephanie said. "It wasn't my fault though. It was my stupid big mouth. I just opened it up and that whole story just flew out before I could stop it."

Jesse stood and shook his head. "I don't know, Stephanie," he said. "I wish I could help you, but I don't know the Spin Masters well enough to ask them a favor."

"That's okay," Stephanie sighed. "It's my problem. I'll figure a way to get out of it." She wished she felt as sure of that as she was trying to sound. *How will I get out of this?* she asked herself.

Jesse leaned over and kissed the top of her head. "I'll tell you what," he said. "I'll help you write a song for the movie."

"Huh?" Stephanie asked.

"Well, if you write the lyrics, I'll come up with the music for it and we can record it down at the studio."

"Really?" she asked.

Jesse shrugged. "Sure. But you'd better work fast, because I don't have much time. I'm a big star, you know. I have important people to see. Important places to go!"

"Jesse!" Becky called down from the attic apartment. "Can you take Alex to the potty?"

Jesse sighed. "Coming!" he yelled.

"But, Uncle Jesse, I can't write a song," she said.

"Why not?" Jesse asked. "You're a writer, right?"

"Yes, but not a songwriter."

Jesse ruffled her hair. "Well, you won't know that until you try."

"Can't you write it?" Stephanie begged. "Please?"

Jesse shook his head. "Too busy," he said. "But

I promise I'll come up with some rockin' music for whatever you write."

"But I told everyone—"

Jesse stopped her. "Listen, Steph, just give it a try, okay? Now I have to get upstairs before Alex—"

"Daddy!" Nicky called from upstairs. "Look what Alex did in the bathroom!"

Jesse made a face, then bolted up the stairs.

Stephanie stared after him and sighed. She'd never be able to write a song. Not one as good as the Spin Masters or Uncle Jesse anyway. How had she gotten herself into this mess? Well, she knew the answer to that. The real question was, would she ever learn her lesson and *not* do it again?

She went upstairs, grabbed a pen and some paper, and flopped down on her bed. Chewing on her pen, she noticed that Peaches the Panda was still wearing the ruffled white shirt.

*I guess I'll give the song a shot*, she thought. *What have I got to lose? But first I have to figure something else out.*

*Who am I going to give the other backstage pass to? Darcy or Allie?*

# Chapter

# 8

◆  ◀  ◾  ◆

Stephanie had been doodling and staring into space for almost an hour when Michelle stuck her head in the room and said, "Phone for you, Stephanie."

Stephanie jumped up eagerly, grateful to have an excuse to get away from her songwriting attempt. She picked up the phone in D.J.'s room and said hello.

"Hi, Stephanie," a male voice said. "It's me."

"Oh, hi, Michael." What could he possibly want?

"Listen, Greg just called me with a good idea for what to film next. He said we should check out the jocks tomorrow. You know, like guys from the football team. They all sit together in the cafeteria, so we'll meet there at lunch."

"Yeah, sure, great idea," Stephanie said. "But why couldn't you tell me this tomorrow in media class?"

"Well, actually, I wanted to ask you something else. . . . Did your uncle get to talk to the Spin Masters yet?"

"I still don't see why this couldn't wait for tomorrow," Stephanie said.

"It's just that I'm starting to wonder, well, worry, really, that you aren't going to come through with the—"

"You don't believe that my uncle knows the Spin Masters?" Stephanie interrupted. "You think I was lying about my uncle and his connections in the music business?"

"Well, no, not exactly," Michael said.

"You thought I was just bragging, didn't you?" Stephanie persisted.

"I didn't say that, Stephanie, I swear. I was only wondering—"

"And did you tell everybody in school that I was a liar?"

"No way," Michael said. "I wouldn't do that. Greg and I were just wondering—"

"Well, you can tell Greg that I was telling the truth. The whole truth and nothing but the truth. And I can prove it to you, Michael. I've got two backstage passes for the Spin Masters show, and since you think I'm such a big liar, I'm going to give one of them to you! Now do you believe me?"

"Wow! Stephanie! Is this for real? Backstage passes?"

"No lie," Stephanie said. "Now, do you want to go or don't you?"

"Definitely!" Michael exclaimed. "I wouldn't miss this for anything. Thanks a whole lot, Stephanie!"

When Stephanie hung up she felt a sense of triumph. "Hah! I guess I showed him!" she said gleefully. "That ought to convince him once and for all that—"

Stephanie stopped and pulled the passes out of her back pocket. "Oh, no! What did I do?"

Stephanie looked at the passes in horror.

"I must be out of my mind! I don't want to go to the concert with Michael! I want to go with Darcy, or Allie, my best friends," she cried.

*Maybe I can call him back and tell him . . . no, then he'd think I was lying again*, Stephanie thought.

Stephanie buried her face in her hands. "I don't believe it," she moaned. "I've done it again! I've just gotten myself in another big mess, and all to impress Michael Allen."

\*  \*  \*

When she met Allie and Darcy at the phone on Thursday morning, Stephanie didn't bring up the backstage passes. She didn't know how she'd explain to her two best friends that she'd given Michael one of the passes. It would have been bad enough if she was forced to choose between one of her friends, but not giving it to either of them was even worse.

"So Jesse never found out about the camera?" Allie asked with concern.

"Whew! What a relief," Stephanie replied.

"We told you it would be cool," Darcy said.

Just then Michael, Greg, and Karen came up to the girls.

"So?" Greg asked. "What did the Spin Masters say?"

Stephanie casually pushed her hair behind her ears and glanced at Darcy and Allie. *Uh-oh*, she thought, *will I have to bring up the backstage passes?*

"Well, I don't know yet," she said to Greg. "My uncle won't see Chris Barton until today. At rehearsal," she added.

"Rehearsal?" Karen asked.

"Oh, didn't I mention?" Stephanie asked innocently. "My uncle's band is opening for the Spin Masters at the concert tomorrow night."

"No way!" Allie said.

"Really?" Darcy asked.

Stephanie couldn't help laughing at the stunned looks on her friends' faces. "He sure is," she said. "For real!" Suddenly Stephanie started feeling pretty good. Soon everyone in school would find out that she really *did* know people in the rock business.

"It's true!" Michael said, smiling at Stephanie. "And Stephanie's taking me to the concert. She's even got backstage passes."

*Oh, no,* Stephanie thought. *Michael and his big mouth.*

"We're still on for tomorrow night, right, Stephanie?" he asked.

"Yup," Stephanie said, trying not to look at Darcy and Allie. When she finally got up the nerve to take a peek, both of them were staring at her with their mouths wide open. They were speechless.

"I can't wait," Michael said.

"So, anyway," Stephanie said, trying to change the conversation, "what about the next part of the movie?"

Michael held up a blank cassette. "We're going to check out that group of guys from the football team at lunch today. You know, get the 'jocks' perspective. We talked about this last night on the phone, Stephanie. Don't you remember?"

Stephanie nodded. She didn't want to be reminded of that horrible phone call. If he had never called, she wouldn't have given him the other pass.

"Good idea," Allie said. "And I think the kids from the Mathletes all sit together at lunch too. So we can interview the 'brains' too."

"That's a great idea, Allie," Stephanie said.

"Oh! Guess what?" Karen said suddenly. "My mom works for the city traffic department and she found out that they are closing some streets in Oakland tomorrow to film a Steven Spielberg movie!"

Darcy's eyes widened. "Get out of here! That's so cool!'"

"My cousin lives there," Allie said. "I wonder if it's close by."

Stephanie suddenly had a fabulous idea. "Michael, maybe you can get Steven Spielberg to be in our movie or something!"

Michael scoffed at the suggestion. "I don't know, Stephanie. He's probably very busy."

"Don't you know him?" Karen asked.

Michael nodded. "Uh-huh. My uncle's worked with him before."

"So maybe you can ask him this weekend at your uncle's wedding!" Stephanie pointed out. This would be so great. If Michael got Steven

Spielberg to help with the movie, then maybe the kids wouldn't be so disappointed in her for not being able to get the Spin Masters.

"Sure, I'll ask him," Michael said.

Just then the first bell rang and the group started to break up.

"Can you just see everyone's faces?" Greg asked excitedly as he walked down the hall. "When Steven Spielberg and the Spin Masters show up in our movie?"

"This is going to be the best media project ever!" Karen added.

"Yeah, the best," Stephanie answered weakly. *Except that there's no way the Spin Masters will be in it.* She tried not to feel sick to her stomach.

As Stephanie, Darcy, and Allie made their way down the hall, Darcy turned to Stephanie and said with a teasing tone, "Looks like you and Michael are a real item now! Backstage passes—wow!"

"Why didn't you tell us about the passes?" Allie asked.

"Well, I got them late last night," Stephanie explained.

"But what time did Michael call?"

"Oh, I forget," Stephanie said. "Listen, you guys, I'm really sorry. I wanted one of you to go with me—both of you to go with me. But somehow, when I was talking to Michael, I just had to give it to him."

"That's okay," Allie said. "We understand if you want to go on a date with Michael."

"Yeah, who wouldn't?" Darcy added.

"But it's not—" Stephanie began to explain.

"It's just that we didn't think you liked him, Stephanie," Allie said with a confused expression on her face. "At least yesterday you said you didn't. And now you're going on a date with him."

"I *don't* like him," Stephanie said, but her words were drowned out by the second bell.

"You're going to have a great time, I'm sure of it!" Darcy said as she took off for homeroom.

"See you later," Allie said. "Let's get together Saturday so you can tell us all about your date!"

# Chapter
# 9

◆ ◀ ◢ ◆

By lunchtime, half the school had already heard about Stephanie's date with Michael and their backstage passes for the Spin Masters.

On her way to the cafeteria, some girls from Stephanie's history class stopped her in the hall.

"Hi, Stephanie!" Mackenzie Sant called out.

Stephanie was surprised the popular eighth grader even knew who she was.

"Hi, Mackenzie," Stephanie said.

"Heard about your date with Michael," Mackenzie said. "That's just so cool!"

Stephanie smiled.

"He was over at your house yesterday?" another girl, Beth Wolf, asked.

Stephanie nodded. "Yeah," she said casually.

"We hung out for a while, then he had to go." She left out the part about four other people being there too.

"He's so cute!" Beth told her. "Everyone thinks so."

Stephanie didn't know what to say to that. "Thanks," she said finally, as if she'd had something to do with his looks.

"What's he like?" Mackenzie asked. "I heard he's really, really sweet."

*Sweet?* Well, that wasn't the first thing that came to Stephanie's mind when she thought about Michael. In fact, it wasn't even the second.

"Yeah, sure, he's sweet," Stephanie replied. "And he's very, um"—come on, Steph! Think of something nice to say!—"uh, talented. Right. He's very talented."

"Wow, you're so lucky!" Beth cooed. "Promise you'll tell us all about your date, okay?"

Stephanie couldn't believe all the attention this whole date thing was getting her. It was kind of unbelievable. Especially since she didn't really like Michael.

"Definitely," Stephanie promised. "Every detail!"

In the cafeteria, Michael, Allie, Karen, and Greg were waiting for her.

"Sorry, guys," Stephanie apologized. "So, let's

get cracking! We don't want to keep the jocks waiting any longer."

Karen laughed. "Should we call them the jocks when we interview them?"

"I don't think so," Allie said. "Let's just call them the athletes."

"Good idea," Stephanie said.

The guys from the football team were all eating the same exact thing for lunch: pizza and orange juice. Stephanie thought this was worth pointing out.

"So, like, how come you guys are all eating the same thing?" she asked one of the guys, Marc Silverberg.

Marc shrugged. "No reason. Just a coincidence," he replied.

"You mean, you didn't realize all nine of you guys were eating pizza today?" Stephanie asked in disbelief.

Marc shook his head. "Nope."

"Do you do other things together, like wear the same clothes and stuff?" Allie asked, hoping to get at least one interesting answer from Marc.

"Unh-unh," Marc replied.

"Well, uh, okay, that's it," Stephanie said. "I don't have any more questions."

Marc shrugged and joined his friends back at the

table. They were all laughing and horsing around as the video crew walked away. Suddenly there was a big uproar, and Stephanie turned around to see what was going on.

At first she didn't recognize Marc Silverberg. That's because he had a pepperoni pizza smeared all over his face—and what was left of the pie in his lap.

"That wasn't much of an interview," Stephanie said when Michael came back over to their table.

"Oh, I got some great footage," Michael insisted. "All you need is the right narration with that, and it'll be a real hoot. You're gonna die when you see it!" he added.

"If you say so," Stephanie said. But privately she wondered just what Michael had in mind.

"So what about the brains?" Greg asked, pointing to a table a few yards away. "Kim Stewart and her friends from Mathletes are sitting over there. We should interview them now."

"Good idea," Michael said.

Stephanie approached Kim and her friends. "Hi, Kim, my name is—"

"You're Stephanie Tanner," Kim said matter-of-factly. "You're the one with backstage passes for the Spin Masters."

Stephanie stared at her in surprise. "How do you know that?" she asked.

Kim shrugged casually. "Oh, it's all over school."

"So anyway, Kim," Stephanie continued, "we're making a movie—"

"For media skills," Kim finished for her. "A documentary, I know. That's all over school too."

Stephanie laughed. "Well, can we interview you guys?"

Kim smiled. "Sure, why not?"

"So, what exactly are Mathletes?" Stephanie asked, putting on her best investigative-reporter voice.

"We're like math athletes," Kim explained. "We play against other schools in math tournaments."

"That's awesome," Allie said. "I should try out for the team. I'm pretty good at math."

"You have to know all kinds of math," Kim told her. "Algebra, trigonometry, calculus."

"Hey, Allie knows her stuff," Stephanie said in support of her friend. "Show her, Allie."

"The square root of the sum of the squares of the sides of a right triangle is equal to the hypotenuse."

"Wow!" Kim said. "I'm impressed! Where did you learn that? Trig? Advanced geometry?"

Allie blushed. "No. *The Wizard of Oz.* The scarecrow says it when he gets his brain from the wizard."

Everybody was laughing, when an ear-splitting siren suddenly sounded throughout the cafeteria.

"What's going on?" Stephanie asked.

Greg and Karen shrugged and gazed around the room.

Just then Stephanie smelled smoke. "Oh, no!" she cried. "I think there's a fire!"

Allie spun around and pointed to the kitchen, where a cloud of thick black smoke came pouring out of the doorway.

Seconds later, cafeteria aides began ushering everyone toward the emergency exits. Soon the entire school filed out the exits and stood in the soccer field behind the cafeteria. Groups of kids all stood around in bunches, and teachers ran back and forth, trying to find out what was going on.

"What's happening?" Darcy wondered.

"Did you see anything?" Allie asked.

"Did anyone see anything?" Stephanie wanted to know.

A few minutes later, Mr. Thomas, the principal, came outside.

"Relax, everyone. Everything is okay," he assured the crowd. "There was a small fire in the kitchen, but it's been extinguished. There was no damage. Everyone is fine. No cause for alarm."

Back inside, all everyone could talk about was the fire. The principal may have called it small, but by the time the story of the grease fire circulated the cafeteria a few times, one would have thought that half of San Francisco had burned to the ground.

Stephanie, Allie, Darcy, Karen, and Greg all met back at their table in the cafeteria. "Hey, where's Michael?" Greg asked.

Stephanie searched the room. "I don't know," she replied. "I saw him out on the soccer field, but I don't see him now. Maybe he's left for his next class or something."

"That's what we should do," Allie said, glancing up at the wall clock.

"Okay. Then we'll meet again tomorrow," Greg said. "In the cafeteria."

"Right," Stephanie replied. "Provided it doesn't go up in flames overnight!"

Later that day Stephanie spied Michael at his locker. He glanced up from his class schedule and said, "Hey, Steph! Where's Allie?"

Stephanie eyed him suspiciously. "She has science this period, why?"

"Oh, no reason. Just that you two are always together. Anyway, that was really something at lunch today, eh?"

"A major event," Stephanie agreed.

Michael reached into his locker and pulled out his history textbook. "Listen, Stephanie, I got some really excellent footage today."

"Yeah?" Stephanie asked. "With all the commotion over the fire, I didn't think you were able to get anything good on Kim and the Mathletes—"

"No, not them!" Michael exclaimed. "Of the fire! Wait till you see it—it's perfect for our documentary!"

"Really?" Stephanie asked in disbelief. "You filmed the actual fire?"

"Yup," Michael answered bravely. "I wasn't scared. I knew there was a story to get, and I went for it! Now all I have to do is go home and edit it on my father's equipment."

"There's a studio here in school," Stephanie said. "We're supposed to learn how to edit film with Mr. Merin next week."

"Don't worry, Stephanie. We'll do the final edit next week like we planned. I'm just getting some scenes in shape early so we'll be sure to make the due date on this project."

Stephanie hesitated. Michael seemed to be doing

some awfully sneaky things with that video camera. "But what exactly will you—"

Michael held up his hand. "Trust me, Steph," he assured her, "you'll love it!"

Stephanie smiled, then left for her health class. For some reason, she didn't trust Michael at all.

# Chapter
# 10

◆ ◀ ◆ ◆

"So here's the thing," Stephanie said to Allie and Darcy the next morning by the pay phone. "The Spin Masters can't do the song."

"Big surprise," Darcy muttered.

"But I know what to do," Stephanie said. "I'm going to write a song. The lyrics, I mean. Uncle Jesse will do the music. So that problem is solved."

"So what's the other problem?" Allie asked.

Stephanie took a deep breath. She didn't know quite how to say this next part. Especially since everyone in the entire school—Allie and Darcy included—thought it was such a big deal.

"The problem is," Stephanie said, "my date tonight with Michael."

Allie stared at her. "Well, I can lend you my

cutoff flannel shirt and maybe Darcy can lend you her black jeans if you—"

Stephanie didn't let her finish. "No, no, no. My problem isn't what to wear. It's something even bigger."

"I thought your aunt was driving you guys to the concert tonight," Darcy said.

"It's not that either," Stephanie said. "Even bigger."

"Well, what is it already?" Allie asked. "What's the big problem?"

Stephanie stared at her two best friends, then blurted it out. "I don't want to go!" she cried. "I don't want to date Michael!"

Allie and Darcy exchanged glances and waited for Stephanie to say more.

Stephanie leaned against the wall and let her backpack fall to the floor. "Okay, here it is," she explained. "A whole week has gone by and I've spent a lot of time with Michael and, well, I have to tell you, I don't think I like him like that."

"But you asked him to go to the concert with you," Allie said.

"It's because he didn't believe me when I said my uncle knew people in the rock business. I had to prove to him that I wasn't bragging, so I gave him the backstage pass. But I wish I hadn't."

Darcy's mouth hung open. "You mean to say you have a date with the cutest guy in school— the guy that half the girls in this school would kill to go out with—and you don't even want to go?"

Stephanie nodded. "That's what I'm saying."

Darcy's hand flew up to her forehead and she pretended to faint. "You're nuts. Certifiably."

"But you said he was gorgeous and everything," Allie said.

"Well, I thought he was," Stephanie said. "When I first met him on Monday, I thought he was gorgeous."

"He still looks the same. It's only Friday," Allie pointed out.

"You said it," Darcy added. "He's still got those beautiful hazel eyes and that to-die-for smile—"

"And those amazingly high cheekbones and adorable dimples," Allie added with a sigh.

"And that gorgeous, thick long hair," Darcy said.

"Okay, already!" Stephanie cried. "I know! He's hot! But it's his personality. I mean, don't you think he's just a bit conceited?"

Darcy shrugged. "I don't know him that well," she said.

Allie thought for a moment. "He does like to talk about himself. But maybe he's just trying to be friendly. He is the new kid, remember? It's never easy being the new kid. Remember when Darcy first tranferred to this school?"

"Oh, that was the worst!" Darcy exclaimed. "It took me three weeks to speak to someone!"

Stephanie and Allie stared at her.

"Okay, well, maybe not three weeks. But it was three days!" She laughed.

Stephanie ran her fingers through her hair and sighed. "I don't know," she said. "He's always talking about being a film director. And he's practically taken over this project."

"And it's a good thing," Allie said. *"Someone's* got to know how to edit the film, or else we'll flunk media. Karen and Greg can use the camera, but they don't know how to edit."

"You're right, but he acts like such a know-it-all."

"But he does know a lot," Allie pointed out. "He's got really creative ideas."

"I guess so," Stephanie said. "But why does he have to brag about his 'Hollywood connections' all the time?"

"Look who's talking about bragging," Allie said, raising her eyebrows. "You got yourself in a major mess by bragging about your rock and roll connections."

"But at least I came through with the passes," Stephanie shot back. "And why are you sticking up for Michael all of a sudden?"

"I'm just saying that you could be a little nicer to Michael, that's all," Allie said calmly. "Just give the new kid a break."

"Okay, okay," Stephanie said. "Sorry."

The warning bell rang and Darcy picked up her books. "So what are you going to do, Stephanie?" she asked.

Stephanie lifted her backpack. "Go on the date, I guess," she said. "Unless you guys have a better idea?" she asked hopefully.

No one said a word.

"Then it looks like I have a date tonight," Stephanie said with a frown. "And instead of being thrilled to go out with the hottest guy in school, I'm wishing I could stay at home and do a fashion show with Michelle and her stuffed animals."

Stephanie stood in front of the open refrigerator and sighed. "I don't want an apple, I don't want leftover spaghetti, I don't want a bagel, and I don't want to go out with Michael tonight."

She closed the refrigerator door and shuffled her way through the living room, where her father was polishing the coffee table.

"So how does it feel to be an eighth-grader, Steph?" Danny asked as he buffed away.

"Michelle doesn't know how good she has it," Stephanie said. "Remember when your biggest problem was what kind of lunchbox was cool?"

"Yeah, those were the days," Danny said wistfully.

"Should you get a Batman lunchbox or a Mighty Morphin Power Rangers lunchbox? What an agonizing decision."

"Actually they hadn't invented Batman or Mighty Morphins yet when I was in third grade," Danny said. Then he frowned and stopped shining the table. "Now that I think of it, they hadn't invented lunchboxes back then either."

Stephanie giggled and continued toward the stairs. Then she stopped abruptly and turned around. She stared at her father incredulously. "Dad?"

"What is it, Steph?"

"Do I see what I think I see?"

"You mean a sparkling clean coffee table? It's amazing, isn't it, what a little muscle will do for this finish. It's so—"

"No, Dad, that's not what I mean. What are you polishing with anyway?"

"Oh, it's this new Spray and Shine Streak Free—"

"Dad! What is that rag in your hand?"

"Oh, this!" Danny said with a chuckle. "Gotta recycle when you can, honey. Why throw away a perfectly good rag?"

"That's not a rag, Dad. Those were my pants. My favorite ripped, torn, and shredded blue jeans. It took them years to get that worn and faded. And now you're using them to clean up coffee rings? How could you?" Stephanie was hoping she'd be able to sneak out of the house one more time with the torn jeans on. They seemed like the perfect thing to wear to the Spin Masters concert.

"I didn't know you were so attached to them, Steph," Danny said. "But they were practically falling off you, you've got to admit. They almost fell apart when I picked them up off your bedroom floor, so it was easy to shred them up into rags."

"Rags?" Stephanie cried, throwing her hands up. "Dad, you just don't get it. They were a work of art."

"Honey, is this anything like that old blanket you used to be attached to? You know, that pink little 'blankey' with all the holes in it that you took with you everywhere when you were three?"

"Forget it, Dad. Just forget it," Stephanie moaned as she walked up to her bedroom.

"On top of everything, now I don't have a clue about what to wear tonight," Stephanie muttered as she collapsed onto the bed.

A few minutes later D.J. passed by, then halted and peered into the room. "Why the long face, Steph? You look as though you've just been dumped."

Stephanie sighed. "Don't I wish. I have another date tonight," she aid.

"You do?" D.J. asked. "With the new kid? A real date this time?"

Stephanie sat up slowly and nodded. "Yeah, with Michael."

"You don't look too happy about it," D.J. pointed out. "I know if I were about to go out with the cutest guy in school, I'd be a little more excited."

"D.J., can I ask you something? Woman to woman?"

D.J. chuckled and sat on the bed. "How about sister to sister?"

"Okay. But it may sound weird," Stephanie warned her.

"Stephanie, weird was when Michelle asked me

at three in the morning if birds sneeze. Is this weirder than that?"

Stephanie laughed. "No."

"Okay, then ask away."

Stephanie took her pillow and clutched it against her chest. "It has to do with guys," she said.

"I figured."

"It's this guy, Michael," Stephanie explained.

"I figured that too," D.J. said.

"Well, all the girls in school have a crush on him. And I guess he likes me. So I should be thrilled, right?"

D.J. nodded.

"Okay, so here's the thing. I'm not thrilled. I'm not even happy. I mean, I was at first, because he's so gorgeous. But now that I know him a little better, I don't really like him all that much. Actually, I think he's one of the most conceited guys I've ever met!"

D.J. sat on the bed next to her sister. "Well—"

"Wait, there's more," Stephanie admitted. "I kind of bragged about Michael to a lot of the girls at school. I guess I was so happy to finally be so popular, I just got carried away. So now everyone thinks I really like him."

D.J. gave an exasperated sigh. "Well, this is a tough one, Steph. I think—"

"Hang on," Stephanie interrupted. "There's more. I also sort of lied. I kept trying to impress him and I kind of told him Uncle Jesse was this bigshot in the music business, just so I'd look cool. So he thinks I have all these rock and roll connections."

D.J. shook her head. "Anything else?" she asked.

"Only that when we're on our date tonight and Michael sees we don't really know the Spin Masters personally, he'll know I lied. And then everyone will find out. I'll be ruined."

D.J. stood and paced the floor of the bedroom. "Steph," she finally said, "remember Rick Casey?"

"Of course," Stephanie replied. "How could I forget him? The exchange student from England that was in your class last year. He's a model now, isn't he?"

D.J. stared dreamily into space. "He sure is." She sighed. "Anyway," she went on, "Rick was the most gorgeous guy I'd ever seen. I couldn't believe he asked me out. I mean, of all the girls in school, he wanted to date me."

"He was cute," Stephanie agreed.

"Right. But he was also dumber than a doorknob," D.J. reminded her. "I was shocked at just how dumb he was. He didn't even know London was the capital of England. And he was born there!

"Anyway, my point is that just because someone is nice-looking doesn't mean he's the perfect guy. Rick and I had the worst two dates ever. Everybody else thought he was such a great catch though. But we had nothing to talk about and I got so sick of him smiling that I'm-smiling-because-I-don't-have-anything-to-say smile all night, that I couldn't wait to get home."

"But Michael isn't dumb," Stephanie pointed out. "He's smart. Very smart. And talented. He's just majorly egotistical."

"Then he's not for you!" D.J. said. "But maybe you should give him a little break. He is new to the school. Maybe he's trying to impress you just like you're trying to impress him. It's hard being the new kid. Believe me, I know. I just started my first year at college. Maybe you shouldn't be so quick to judge."

"I guess you're right. But what am I supposed to do now? He'll be here in half an hour!" Stephanie fretted.

"Tell him the truth," D.J. stated. "Not the part about him being egotistical, of course, but just that you'd rather be good friends. Honesty is the most important thing, Stephanie."

Stephanie buried her face in her pillow. D.J. was

right. Honesty was the most important thing. She had to tell Michael the truth. About everything.

The knot in her stomach felt a little looser.

*Now all I have to do is come up with something to wear,* Stephanie thought as she rummaged through her drawers. *And not the same old thing I wear to school every day. Something special, but sort of casual.*

Stephanie opened one drawer after another, then surveyed what was hanging in her closet. The flowered skirt was too dressy, but jeans and a sweater was so boring. Stephanie sat on her bed and stared at the wall.

Peaches the Panda stared back.

"Peaches. Peaches, my old friend. What are you wearing?"

Stephanie stood up and climbed onto Michelle's bed, where the stuffed Panda sat among countless other fuzzy animals. "Could it be?" Stephanie whispered. She took a closer look and said, "Michelle, you're a lifesaver."

"I am?" Michelle said, coming into the room and looking up at her sister.

"Those are my ripped-up jeans you've got on Peaches, aren't they?"

"Yup," Michelle said. "I found them in the basement. Dad cut off the legs to use as rags. Don't they make cute shorts?"

111

"The cutest. You've saved them from a horrible fate. Dad would probably use them to wash the car, or, worse, the dog. And now I can wear them tonight. Over a pair of cotton tights. They'll be perfect."

"But what about Peaches?"

"You know, I never realized what great fashion sense you had," Stephanie said. Maybe if she flattered her sister, Michelle wouldn't mind so much that she was undressing her panda.

"They fit Peaches perfectly," Michelle said, pleased with herself.

"And that ruffled shirt is just right with those cutoff shorts, Michelle!"

"You're going to wear that blouse too?" Michelle asked with a slight frown. "I thought you gave that to me."

"It's just what I was looking for," Stephanie said excitedly. "It's a really cool combination."

Michelle beamed.

Stephanie took the ruffled shirt off the panda and put it on herself.

"Michelle, you're a fashion genius!" Stephanie said.

"I know," Michelle said with a grin from ear to ear.

# Chapter
# 11

♦ ◀ ▸ ♦

"Stephanie!" Danny Tanner called out. "Michael is here!"

Stephanie clutched her hairbrush to her chest and stared at her reflection in the bathroom mirror.

"Okay, Dad!" she yelled. "I'll be right down!"

Stephanie paced the bathroom floor, still gripping the hairbrush.

"Be honest," she told herself. "D.J. said be honest. I have to tell Michael the truth. That I like him as a friend, that the eight-millimeter camera isn't mine and that I lied about the Spin Masters."

She gulped. "Okay, maybe I won't put it quite like that." Stephanie looked in the mirror and rehearsed. "Michael, I wasn't entirely honest about my connections with the Spin Masters."

However she put it, she knew it wasn't going to be easy.

Stephanie finally let go of the brush and checked her outfit one last time. Nothing too trendy or funky—just a pair of cutoff jeans and a white shirt. From now on she was going to dress more honestly too. *Dad probably won't notice the cutoffs*, Stephanie figured, *now that all the holes are gone.*

Downstairs Michael sat on the sofa while Danny hovered over, firing questions at him.

"So, Michael," Danny asked. "Where are you taking my daughter tonight?"

"Well, actually," Michael answered nervously, "Stephanie is taking me out tonight. To the concert."

"Oh, right, right," Danny said. "And when will you be home?"

Michael's voice shook. "When it's over?" he asked.

"That's right," Danny said, narrowing his eyes at Michael. "The second it's over, you come straight home!"

"But—"

"You have a problem with that, young man?" Danny demanded.

Michael swallowed hard. "Uh, no, Mr. Tanner.

It's just that you're picking us up from the concert."

Stephanie laughed as she came down the stairs. "Dad, go easy on him, okay? Aunt Becky is taking us to the concert and we'll be with her or Uncle Jesse. So stop worrying."

Danny eyed his daughter suspiciously. "And you'll meet me in the parking lot afterward?"

"For the millionth time, yes!"

"Okay, kids!" Becky announced as she came running down the stairs. "Let's roll!"

"Aunt Becky, this is Michael. Michael, this is my aunt."

Michael smiled. "I already know you," he said. "I watch *Wake Up, San Francisco* all the time. I'm a big fan of—"

"Oh, that's sweet!" Danny said. "Would you like an autographed picture?" He grabbed a pen.

Michael's eyes lit up. "You mean it? I can have an autographed picture of Rebecca Donaldson? Wow, my parents will freak out! We're all big fans." He noticed Danny's hurt expression. "Oh, of course you too, Mr. Tanner," he added.

Danny shuffled awkwardly. "Oh, sure, I knew that."

Stephanie grabbed Michael by the arm. "Come on, let's go. We don't want to miss Uncle Jesse."

*And I don't want my father to have time to inspect my outfit,* she added silently.

On the way to the concert Stephanie wrung her hands together so tightly, she nearly stopped her blood circulation. She and Michael barely said a word to each other in the car. All she could think about was what she was going to say to him, playing it over and over in her mind. And each time she played it, she grew more and more nervous.

At the park there were cars everywhere. The place was jam-packed. Becky parked and they all went backstage to find Jesse. It took them a while to find the backstage entrance, through a maze of long halls.

Michael kept touching the pass that hung on a string around his neck. Stephanie was sure he was trying to show it off in front of the people around them. It made her totally uncomfortable.

Finally they made it backstage, and Becky was allowed to go to Jesse's dressing room. Stephanie and Michael were given chairs to sit on behind the stage next to several other fans.

They sat in silence for a few minutes. Stephanie pretended to be interested in watching the roadies set the stage. The curtain was closed, so she couldn't see the crowd in the amphitheater.

Finally Michael broke the silence.

"So, Stephanie, did your uncle talk to Chris Barton?"

Stephanie stared at the floor, twisting the ring on her finger. *It's now or never*, she thought, taking a deep breath.

"Well, to tell you the truth," she said, "I kind of wasn't being completely honest about that."

Michael stared at her. "What do you mean? I thought you said your uncle knew them."

"He does, now, sort of. But he didn't know them then, and he still doesn't know them well enough to make them write a song for us."

"You mean you lied?"

Stephanie swallowed hard. "Kind of," she said.

"What for?" Michael asked.

Stephanie shrugged. "I don't know. I just got caught up in the whole movie thing, I guess. I'm sorry!"

Michael shook his head again. "What are you going to tell the others?" he asked. "They were counting on the Spin Masters."

"Well, we still have Steven Spielberg," Stephanie reminded him.

Suddenly Michael blushed and looked away.

"Michael, what is it? Are you okay?"

"Yes! I'm fine," he snapped, trying to avoid her stare.

But Stephanie wasn't fooled. "You don't know Steven Spielberg!" she cried. "You don't know him at all!"

Michael didn't say anything.

"So you lied too!" Stephanie felt a wave of relief. "Do you even have an uncle?" she asked.

"Yes!" Michael insisted. "And he's a director, only . . . he isn't as famous as I said."

"Why did you say he was?" Stephanie asked. "How come you said that stuff about him and Arnold Schwarzenegger and Steven Spielberg?"

Michael thought for a moment. "I guess I was trying to impress you and the others. I was nervous about fitting in at a new school," he admitted.

Stephanie stared at him in disbelief. "You?"

"Yeah, me. Why is that so hard to believe?"

"Because you seem so outgoing," she told him. "You don't look like the sort of guy who would have a problem making friends."

Michael shrugged. "Well, I do."

Stephanie suddenly felt sorry for Michael. Though it was hard for her to believe someone as cute as Michael would have trouble making new friends, she supposed it was possible.

"Michael, you're a really talented filmmaker," Stephanie said in all seriousness. "The stuff you've done for the movie so far is awesome."

"You really think so?" Michael asked.

"Definitely," Stephanie replied. "I mean, you don't have to go making up stories to get kids to like you. People will see how talented you are and like you for *you*—not for who you know. Honesty, after all, is the most important thing."

Stephanie suddenly realized what she'd just said and nearly burst out laughing.

"What's so funny?" Michael asked.

"It's just that my sister D.J. said the exact same thing to me about a half hour ago!"

Michael laughed too. "Well, it must be good advice, then."

Stephanie smiled. Michael wasn't so bad after all. In fact, he was sort of sweet.

"Well, since we're telling the whole truth, my uncle did ask the Spin Masters to do our song. Only they were too busy. But—" she paused dramatically—"I'm going to write us a song."

"You?" he asked in surprise.

"I'll write the words. My uncle said he'd come up with the melody," she replied.

"You can write a song?" Michael seemed impressed.

"I can try," she said.

"This is great!" Michael looked relieved too. "But what do we do now?" he asked her. "I mean, we have to tell the others about the Spin Masters and Steven Spielberg."

"Tell you what," Stephanie said. "Let's just tell the others that the arrangements fell through. That sounds like Hollywood."

Michael stared at her. "Yeah?" he asked.

Stephanie smiled. "Yeah, it'll be our secret."

"You mean you won't tell anybody?" Michael asked.

"Nope. I promise." She held up her hand, indicating scout's honor.

"Not even Allie?" Michael asked.

Stephanie shook her head. "Tell me something, Michael," she said. "Why do you ask so many questions about Allie?"

Michael smiled his lopsided smile.

"You like her, don't you!" Stephanie laughed, poking him in the arm with her finger. "I knew it!" she added. "But why did you ask me out, then?"

Michael grinned again. "Well, I thought if I got to know you better, you would like me enough to fix me up with Allie!"

Stephanie laughed. "But now half the school thinks we're going out!"

Michael's eyes widened. "Seriously?"

Stephanie nodded. "Oh, yeah. We're the talk of the school."

"Well, will you?" Michael asked.

"Will I what?"

"Fix me up with Allie!" Michael said.

"No," she said with a serious expression.

Michael looked hurt. "Why not?"

Stephanie smiled and said, "You can ask her yourself. You asked me out, didn't you?"

"Yeah, but I didn't like you the way I like Allie."

"Well, I have a feeling Allie likes you the way you like her, so go ahead and ask."

"Hey, look!" Michael pointed to the stage. "The concert's starting!"

Stephanie gazed up onstage and squealed with delight. "That's my uncle!" she cried as Jesse and his band took the stage.

"That guy in the leather jacket is your uncle?" Michael asked.

Stephanie nodded proudly. "Yup." Then she remembered something.

"Uh, Michael? Since we're being totally honest here, I have another confession to make."

"What's that, Stephanie?"

"The camera," she explained, "the eight millimeter. It, uh, isn't mine. It's my uncle's."

She waited for him to lace into her for lying, but instead he began to laugh.

"Don't worry," he told her. "The camera I have isn't exactly mine either. It's my dad's!"

Up onstage, Jesse walked up to the microphone. "Hello, San Francisco!" he screamed. His voice echoed through the air. Stephanie and Jesse watched as thousands of people started screaming and cheering. Becky came over and started clapping and cheering too.

Stephanie watched in amazement as her uncle played his first song and hundreds of people got up and danced.

"They like him," she said breathlessly.

Michael grinned. "He's pretty good," he said. "Wanna dance?"

Stephanie smiled, then decided it was time to have fun. She and Michael danced and laughed all through Jesse's gig, and all through the Spin Masters. And when the night was nearing the end, Stephanie decided she'd had a really nice time. Michael wasn't such a bad guy after all.

He'd be perfect for Allie.

# Chapter

# 12

◆ ◀ ◢ ◆

"So what do you think?" Stephanie asked Jesse after reading him her song. It was Saturday afternoon, and Stephanie had spent most of the day working on the lyrics.

Jesse didn't answer.

"Uncle Jesse?" At that moment Stephanie knew she should never have agreed to write a song. It was awful. Her uncle's face said it all. What did she know about songwriting anyway?

"That bad, eh?" she asked, hanging her head.

"Oh, no, Stephanie!" Jesse exclaimed. "Your song was unbelievable! It's just that it left me—wow!—speechless."

Stephanie's eyes widened. "Really?" she asked.

"Really!" Jesse assured her. "If I'd known you

could write lyrics like that, I would have had you write a song for my band a long time ago."

Jesse jumped up from his desk and took his acoustic guitar from the closet.

"You really think it's good?" Stephanie asked again.

"I wouldn't lie, Steph. Now, let's see what I can do with it. I was thinking something slow, with a rock and roll beat. Something Lisa Loeb-ish."

"Great! I love her."

Jesse fiddled around with some chords for a while, then began to sing Stephanie's song, "Don't Judge a Book." When he got to the chorus, Stephanie sang along with him.

> "So don't ever judge a book
> Always take a deeper look
> You may be surprised at what you find
> When you read between the lines
>
> So don't ever judge a book
> Always take a deeper look
> And when the story comes to an end
> You may just find you have a friend."

Stephanie jumped up and applauded when Jesse hit the last chord. "That sounded great, Uncle

Jesse. I mean the music part. Are you sure the words aren't dumb?"

Jesse put down his guitar. "Now, would I like a song with dumb words?" he asked.

Stephanie smiled. Then she remembered the words to his beloved "Hound Dog." "You like a song about a dog that's always crying. Why does that dog cry all the time anyway?"

"Okay, okay, I get your point." Jesse laughed. "But that was a big hit. And anyway, your lyrics are much, much better, not to disrespect the King or anything."

"Thanks, Uncle Jesse," Stephanie laughed. "But this song has to be awesome. Awesome enough to make everyone forget the Spin Masters."

Jesse picked up his guitar again. "Well, then we have a lot of work ahead of us," he said. "By Monday, I promise, you'll have a number one hit to take to class!"

That night Stephanie got Allie and Darcy on the phone for a three-way call. She told them everything—all about her talk with D.J., her fashion consultation with Michelle and Peaches, the Spin Masters and Uncle Jesse's band, and that she had a great time with Michael.

"You did?" Allie said.

"Yes, I did," Stephanie said. "And you know what, Allie? You were right about him. He *is* a nice guy. He was just trying a little too hard, that's all."

"Did you tell him that the Spin Masters can't write the song?" Allie asked.

"Yup, and I told him that I would write it. Which is what I've been doing all day."

"So when do we get to hear your song?" Darcy asked.

"Why don't we all meet at the mall tomorrow and I'll bring a tape with me," Stephanie said.

"What did Michael say when you told him you were lying all along about the Spin Masters?" Darcy said.

Stephanie explained that Michael was really cool about it, and that he admitted he'd been lying himself. "He also admitted something else to me, Allie."

"What are you talking about, Stephanie?"

"Oh, just a little secret between Michael and me," Stephanie said slyly.

"Stephanie, we've had enough of your secrets this week to last us through all of eighth grade," Allie said. "And maybe through eight more years of higher education. Now, tell us what you're talking about—now!"

"Let's just say that a certain gorgeous new boy

who happens to be creative and charming might be asking you out on a real date—real soon."

"Are you for real?"

"Would I lie to you?" Stephanie said.

"You don't want me to answer that," Allie said with a laugh.

"Speaking of honesty," Stephanie said, "I've decided to tell Jesse that I borrowed his video camera without telling him. Only the truth from now on."

"So does that mean you're going to tell your father you wore those cutoff shorts to the concert?" Darcy asked. "Since he didn't notice them in the car."

"Well, let's not get too carried away with this honesty thing," Stephanie replied. "Sometimes what you don't know won't hurt you."

A week later Stephanie sat nervously in the front row of media skills as Mr. Merin wheeled a big-screen television into the room.

This was it. The day their video would make its debut in front of the class. Stephanie, Allie, Michael, Karen, and Greg had spent the whole week editing in the school's studio. After they had all heard Stephanie's song, they took a vote and decided to change the name of the film to *Don't Judge a Book*. Now Stephanie was so nervous and excited, her stomach made truly weird gurgling noises. She spun around in her chair and spotted Michael sitting in the back of the room with Greg and Karen. She waved at them and held up a pair of crossed fingers.

"This is so exciting!" Allie whispered in her ear. "Do you know I heard Mr. Merin say if he liked our video, he would enter it in a state competition?"

"No way!" Stephanie exclaimed.

"Really," Allie told her. "He told me this morning. Wouldn't that be so cool?"

Stephanie nodded. "Very," she said. "People all around San Francisco would hear my song. I'd be famous!"

"And Michael too," Allie pointed out.

Stephanie smiled. "Excited about your date with Michael tonight?" she asked.

Allie nodded.

"He's really a great guy, Al," Stephanie told her. "You'll have fun."

"Oh, that reminds me," Allie said. "Michael told me to tell you he re-edited a little piece of the movie last night."

"He did?" Stephanie asked. "Why? Which part?"

Allie shrugged. "I don't know, he said it's a surprise."

"Well, I'm sure it will be great," Stephanie told her. "Everything Michael did with this video is great."

Allie nodded in agreement. It was certainly true. Michael had turned a simple class project into one of the coolest films Stephanie had ever seen. He really was incredibly talented. And her entire class was about to see just how talented.

Mr. Merin cleared his throat and leaned casually on the big TV. "Our first project will be presented by the video group. Stephanie? Would you like to tell the class about your group project?"

Stephanie stood and faced her classmates. "I could tell you what our video project is about," she said. "But it would be much more fun to show you!" With that, she pressed play on the VCR and returned to her seat. "The name of the movie is *Don't Judge a Book*."

"Welcome to the cafeteria," a voice boomed. Immediately, the entire class began to laugh. Instead of the school cafeteria, Michael had edited in footage of prisoners being served mush for lunch in jail.

Stephanie gazed around the room, examining the faces of her classmates as they watched. Everyone seemed glued to the set. And they were laughing in all the right places.

"In the cafeteria you'll find a wide variety of people," the film announcer—Stephanie—went on. "People who bring their lunch, people who buy their lunch, and even people who wear their lunch." The class cracked up again as they watched Marc Silverberg from the football team get covered in pizza by his teammates.

Stephanie leaned back in her chair. She didn't need to watch the movie—she'd seen it a hundred times already. It had turned out great. She was happy the others hadn't been too upset about not getting the Spin Masters for the sound track or Steven Spielberg for the narration. Well, at first they had been disappointed, but they'd gotten over it.

The entire class suddenly broke up into gales of laughter. It was the part where Michael had interviewed the cafeteria cooks, then edited in film clips of the Three Stooges fighting and throwing pies at each other. That part always cracked her up too.

When the class erupted in laughter again, Stephanie watched the scene with Courtney and the cheerleaders. Michael had agreed to take out the mean parts and leave in only the really funny stuff. He'd taken out the part where Courtney's squadmate had said nasty things about her, and put in some funny footage taken from last weekend's football game. After Courtney said that the cheer-leaders were all one big happy family, she and her squadmate were shown fighting over a pom-pom. It was pretty hilarious.

When Stephanie heard the first chords of "Don't Judge a Book" at the end of the video, she straight-ened in her seat. This was it. The big moment. She couldn't believe how nervous she was.

The ending was definitely the best part of the film. Michael had managed to get some amazing footage the day of the cafeteria fire. He filmed Kim Stewart from Mathletes choking from the smoke and Marc Silverberg, the jock, coming to her rescue. Stephanie and Allie had written in the script all this mushy stuff about people pulling together in a crisis. She had to admit, it was pretty touching stuff.

Then, just when the last scene was supposedly over, a voice—Michael's voice—came on. Steph-anie didn't remember this part, and she looked on curiously.

"The cafeteria is a strange and wonderful place indeed," he said. "You never know who you might meet. That jock at the next table might turn out to be a Mathlete too. And that cheerleader across from you might turn out to be on the honor roll.

"And that regular kid? Well, that regular kid might just turn out to be a rock and roll singer in disguise. So remember—don't judge a book by its cover."

Stephanie gasped in horror when she saw what appeared on-screen. Her jaw dropped open and she leaned forward in her seat, staring in disbelief at the TV.

"Oh, my—" The words got caught in her throat. She could do nothing but stare at the TV.

On-screen, a messy-haired Stephanie was jumping up and down, singing into a hairbrush. In the background, her four-year-old cousins banged drumsticks, blew into kazoos, and danced around her. Comet, Becky, and Jesse were also there. Stephanie's classmates rolled in the aisles with laughter. She covered her eyes with her hands and sank lower and lower in her chair. What she really wished was that she could crawl under her desk and die.

"I'll get you for this, Michael Allen!" she yelled across the room. But a tiny smile appeared on her face all the same.

After all, it *was* pretty funny!

**Join the gang—and spend sixteen months with your favorite characters from the hit TV show <u>FULL HOUSE</u>!**

# FULL HOUSE™

## 1995-1996 CALENDAR

D.J., Stephanie, Michelle, Uncle Jesse—even Comet—are all here in your very own calendar to get you through the school year and beyond!

Filled with photos from all eight seasons of the hit sitcom, this calendar has plenty of room for you to add your own important dates! Keep track of birthdays, parties, and family gatherings while you watch your favorite characters grow-up over the years!

## From Minstrel® Books
Published by Pocket Books

™ & © 1995 Warner Bros. Television                    1096-01

A series of novels based on your favorite
character from the hit TV show!

# FULL HOUSE ™
# Stephanie

**Available from Minstrel® Books
Published by Pocket Books**

™ & © 1993, 1994, 1995 Warner Bros. Television. All Rights Reserved.   929-09

# FULL HOUSE™
# Michelle

## #1:THE GREAT PET PROJECT

## #2: THE SUPER-DUPER SLEEPOVER PARTY

## #3: MY TWO BEST FRIENDS

## #4: LUCKY, LUCKY DAY

Based on the Hit TV Series!

Available from

A MINSTREL® BOOK

Published by Pocket Books

™ & © 1994, 1995 Warner Bros. Television  All Rights Reserved.  1033-07